The Owl Prince

Green Labyrinth: Book One

ALEX FAURE

To A. G.

AUTHOR'S NOTE

The events and individuals described in these pages are fictitious. The broader historical context, however, is real. In A.D. 82, during the reign of Emperor Domitian, the Romans occupied England and Wales, in addition to much of the known world. Roman Britain was under the command of Governor Gnaeus Julius Agricola, a general who subdued the fractious tribes and made incursions into Scotland (then called Caledonia). It was an era in which the Empire was nearing its high water mark, which would be followed by a slow and inevitable decline. While there is little evidence to suggest that the Romans invaded the island they called Hibernia, and which we now know as Ireland, I've taken the liberty of imagining a world in which they did.

CHAPTER ONE

Summer, 82 A.D.

Darius nodded, and his men forced the Celts to their knees.

It had become a familiar routine, though they'd never captured a group this size before. The Celts who inhabited this green, haunted island fought to the death, or not at all. Darius had seen only a handful flee before the Roman onslaught in the four months he had served in Hibernia. And yet today they had captured twenty enemy warriors and dragged them back to the fort with little effort and no loss of Roman life.

Another triumph to add to Rome's list of early successes in this far-flung backwater.

"Captain?" Darius said to his second, Marcus Lentulus.

"We caught them spying on the fort, Commander," Marcus replied. "Armed with bows and arrows. Likely hoping to pick off the next group of surveyors we sent out into the forest. Like last time."

Darius paced before the Celts, his gaze running over each face. Some of the captives were enormous—the Celts were larger, on average, than most Romans, not that it mattered. Most were fair, their hair ranging from wheat-pale to a rich, deep gold that caught the sunlight shafting through the clouds and gave them an almost holy appearance. They wore close-fitting trousers and tunics, which were filthy, covered in dirt and blood.

Darius stopped before one, a youth with hair as red as ripe berries. Darius had never seen hair that colour before coming to these lands at the edge of the Empire. He suppressed an urge to reach out a hand to touch it.

The young man stared back at him, his eyes an equally strange shade of grey-green, the colour of the sea around Cyprus. His moon-pale skin was spattered with brown marks—some suitably violent form of freckles, Darius guessed. Possibly a disease.

Darius forced his gaze to the next captive. He didn't believe the stories—that the Celts on this island, unlike the motley but tractable tribes of Britannia, were closer to wild beasts than men, the descendants of savage dryads who peopled the endless green forests. Yet gazing into a face that strange, he wasn't surprised by how easily such stories spread.

He stopped before a dark-haired boy who wouldn't meet his eyes. With one finger, Darius lifted his chin. The boy, who was trembling lightly, raised his pale eyes to meet Darius's dark ones.

Darius knew how he must look to the boy—fierce and glowering in his armour, taller than most Romans, a man not yet thirty with the weight of an Empire at his back. Or, at least, that of the 7000-strong force of Romans stationed at three newly built forts along the Eastern Hibernian coast, the first wave of many.

Darius saw his suspicions confirmed in the boy's face. The Celts, bestial barbarians that they were, often sent children into battle in lieu of men. Darius didn't permit the capture of men younger than sixteen. He guessed this one to be fourteen at most.

"Release him," Darius said, removing his hand from the boy's chin. The soldiers moved to comply. "Give him food and water and turn him out of the fort. And that one."

"Commander?" Marcus blinked at the man Darius indicated, a yellow-haired Celt with a murderous gaze. "He isn't—"

"No," Darius agreed. "But he has a deformity in his foot. It would have hindered his abilities. His choice to fight in spite of the handicap brings him honour. His capture brings us none. Release him."

The men complied good-naturedly, being used to such directives from their idiosyncratic commander by now. The soldiers of Sylvanum were in a good mood. They'd finished construction on the fort only four days ago, and the nights since had been filled with merriment.

Marcus, after a short, reluctant pause, nodded, his grimace imperfectly suppressed.

Darius eyed him. While the soldiers might be used to Darius's unusual style of command by now, Marcus had been at Sylvanum only a week, after a stint at Attervalis, the fort to the north.

"Captain Lentulus?" Disdain crept into Darius's voice. If a man had something to say, he should come out and say it, even if it would cause his superior officer to fly into a rage.

Marcus pressed his lips together. He saluted, then left to attend to his duties. Suppressing his irritation, Darius turned to give instructions regarding the remaining captives. He watched as the Celts were led away. They would be questioned by the translator tomorrow, and then executed.

One of those Celts, his balance upset by his bound hands and feet, stumbled against the well. His bonds mustn't have been secured tightly, for his hand came free, and he steadied himself against the moist stone, his head bowed over the water as if yearning for a drink. The Roman guarding him merely helped him find his feet and secured his hands again. No captive had ever suffered a beating at Sylvanum—another of Darius's orders. What was the use in hitting dead men?

"What do you make of it?" said Scipio, Darius's former second. He was a red-faced man in his middle forties, philosophically good-natured, and had served with Darius in both Britannia and Gaul. He had taken his demotion in stride, making way for Marcus, the hero of a recent series of skirmishes that had pushed the enemy tribes of Hibernia into further retreat.

Darius had been less philosophical when he'd received the news, delivered on the last ship from Britannia and written in Governor Agricola's own hand. Darius didn't want some green soldier on his first mission abroad acting as his second, regardless of how well he swung a sword. Sylvanum might not be the largest of the three Hibernian forts—that was Undanum. But Sylvanum was the most precariously situated, hemmed in by dense forest on all sides, while Undanum and Atteralis perched on rocky sea cliffs.

"Likely a breakaway force," Darius said, his thoughts still on Marcus. "It was certainly not a planned attack."

"I wouldn't quite call it an attack, as it was our forces who discovered them. Are the elves capable of planning?" Scipio said it with a snort, using the latest epithet to gain currency among the men. 'Elf' was a loanword from one of the Germanic tribes for a race of leafy beings with little sense but ample malevolence.

"They're Robogdi," Darius said darkly. "We don't know what they're capable of."

The Robogdi, led by the feral King Culland, were the most troublesome of Hibernia's enemy tribes, having attacked several Roman expeditions. They had an established feud with the Darini, the Empire's allies, whose king had extended Agricola the invitation to invade. King Culland might call himself the King of Hibernia, but he was a pretender to the title. The true King of Hibernia was Giareth of the Darini, servant of Agricola and the Emperor Domitian. Eventually, the Hibernian tribes would accept this, and bow to him as one people. But until then, there would be problems, messy ones.

We need more men.

It wasn't the first time Darius had thought it. Rome had been in Hibernia less than a year, and it often seemed that the island occupied little of Agricola's attention. The general was convinced that Hibernia would be an easy conquest. Darius rarely disagreed with Agricola, but in this case, he found himself questioning his judgment.

"All the elves look alike to me," Scipio said. "How can you tell they're Robogdi?"

"The Robogdi are fairer, on the whole." Darius said it absently. "Golden hair. Eyes like the sea off the coast of Epirus. Did you say our men discovered *them*?"

"Yes. Marcus came upon them standing in a clearing, staring through the trees at our men like startled owls. They tried to fight their way out, of course, but Marcus had them surrounded."

Darius frowned, a little shiver going down his back. "He caught them by surprise?"

"From the sounds of it. Marcus isn't the type to downplay his accomplishments, so I took him at his word."

Darius watched the last of the Celts disappear in the direction of the prison block. "Station additional sentries on the walls tonight. And instruct the senior officers to gather in my quarters in two hours."

Scipio nodded slowly. "It doesn't smell right, does it?"

"No."

Darius had served two years in Britannia before being transferred to Hibernia to oversee the construction of Sylvanum. Rome had so far fought no battles with the Hibernians, only skirmishes—perhaps that was all the barbarians could muster, given that their island was divided into multiple warring kingdoms. Darius knew the Celts to be an ethereal people, with the ability to fade in and out of their interminable forests like a breath of wind. On several occasions, while leading men through those dark lands, Darius had sensed eyes upon him. Turning, he had met the gaze of a Celt peering out from behind a tree a few paces away, a Celt who had evidently been trailing them for some time, undetected by any of Darius's scouts.

Scipio was watching him. "Do you think it's safe to hold them here?"

Darius considered it. He had learned never to assume that you could predict a Celt, which meant nothing, and everything. "Execute them immediately."

"The light's fading. We won't be have time to—"

"Leave the bodies for the wolves." Darius strode away, leaving Scipio fumbling over a hasty salute.

Darius paused at the gate, which had remained open following the return of his soldiers. Up in the watchtower, several men were singing as they raised the Roman standard over the new fort. Beyond the gate lay a peaceful meadow that separated Sylvanum from the immensity of the forest. The sun shone, gleaning off the wings of insects that hung in the air like a glittering spell. Behind them, a dark wall of trees.

It was familiar, this Hibernian scene—beauty and savagery, intrinsically linked. Darius could hear the nearby river slicing its way through the dusky woods, chasing its own foamy rivulets to a chasm, all that weight of water thundering against earth and stone. Darius had seen that river, had stumbled and torn his way through those forests with his men on exploratory surveys.

One more year.

Rome ensured its soldiers had comfortable retirements, and Darius was nearing the end of his twelve-year service, having joined the Empire's ranks at the youngest possible age. He thought of the short, docile trees in the Sicilian hills where he had spent his youth. The dry wind, which carried the scent of terracotta and sun-warmed earth.

Darius's hand tightened on the hilt of his sword. He had no one waiting for him. His beloved father was dead, and he had no siblings. A meaningless string of lovers but no wife. He had no absent companions to yearn for, and so he put his yearning into the idea of the land itself, its smell and sound and taste, sensual as any lover.

It was all he had. It was enough.

One more year on this green island. He would help Agricola build more forts and tame the tribes, cementing Roman rule in Hibernia. Then, at long last, he would make his way back to Sicily. His father's olive groves, where he had gamboled as a boy, and spent long days napping and reading in their shade, now belonged to him. He would not leave them again.

Darius glanced down at his hand, tight on his sword hilt. The scars that criss-crossed his knuckles stood out in stark relief.

He motioned to the men, and they closed the gate against the gathering dark.

CHAPTER TWO

Darius strode through the barracks. The air was sweet with celebratory triumph—every soldier seemed to have a smile on his face. Darius found his mood lightening as he walked. As an experienced officer of Rome, he'd seen both good and bad times, and knew to cherish the former whenever he could. The new fort was beautiful, in its practical Roman way, all tidy lines and sharp angles, a testament to the might and ingenuity of the Empire.

It was full dark now, and Darius paused for a quick wash and a shave in the Spartan baths before completing his survey of the defenses. He could have left it to Marcus, he supposed, but habit kept him on his guard at all times.

Habit, and something more than that. The Celts' bizarre capture was a riddle in want of a solution. The executions had been carried out without a hitch, the bodies deposited at the forest's edge. Their plans, if they had any, had been taken with them to the grave.

He pushed back his frustration as he stepped through the door to the officers' quarters. His footsteps thudded against the rough stone floor. Gradually, he became aware of something else.

The sound of carnal pleasure.

Darius frowned. Had one of the officers left his door open? Darius had no objection to his soldiers seeking pleasure in each other—campaigns were long, after all, and Darius well understood the demands of the flesh—provided they did so discreetly. Yet this couple was making enough noise to wake the dead. Were they drunk?

Darius followed the noises to a little-used corridor. There he found, half-hidden in a shadowy alcove, two men locked together, one driving hard into the other.

The closest man—a centurion called Evander—was fully clothed, having merely lifted his skirt above his waist, while his smaller partner was naked save for his boots, his clothes scattered as if they had been haphazardly torn off. The smaller man's hand was at his own cock as Evander held his hips and fucked him. He was emitting lustful moans, and pushing back sinuously against Evander as the bigger man pummelled him, flesh slapping against flesh.

As Darius stood there, wondering vaguely what to do, the moans reached a crescendo, and the naked man came messily across the flagstones. Evander let out a low cry, and his body spasmed, driving one last time into his partner.

Darius stepped forward, expecting the two men to jump to attention, red-faced and stammering, at the sound of his boots. Instead, the naked man turned and began caressing the other. It was Gaius, a young recruit from one of the northern provinces.

As Darius watched, Evander pushed Gaius against the wall, kissing him with an almost violent passion. Gaius murmured something into his mouth. Evander, unbelievably, was already hardening again.

Darius retreated, disquieted. Evander and Gaius continued to display an utter obliviousness to his presence, though he made no effort to quiet his steps. As he put distance between himself and them, he heard Gaius's moans recommence.

It wasn't the first time that Darius had seen men, long cooped up in hostile outposts and separated from their wives and lovers back home, demonstrate similar abandonment when finally allowed the release of sex. But he hadn't known Gaius appreciated men. In fact, he understood him to be stridently on the opposite side, based on overheard gossip from soldiers who had tried to tempt him. Darius had never understood men of that inclination—he himself bedded any partner who was attractive and willing. He had once flirted outrageously with a blushing courtesan in a tavern, only to feel, after they retired to her quarters, something hard pressing against him. He had fucked her anyway, and enjoyed himself no less for the surprise.

Well. Clearly Evander had landed on a convincing argument.

Darius would speak to them both in the morning. Evander and Gaius were good men, and Darius doubted they would require more than a reprimand to encourage them to be more circumspect in future.

As he strode into the briefing room, a low-ceilinged space anchored by a sturdy table, the officers snapped to attention. Darius nodded his greeting.

"Well?" he said, pouring himself a cup of wine. He added a generous amount of water. He wanted a clear head.

"Our scouts found nothing, Commander," Marcus said, speaking before the more seasoned men could open their mouths. It was his right, as second, yet still Darius found himself suppressing irritation. Marcus was the sort of man who could inspire antipathy while rescuing a horse from a burning barn. "There's no evidence of some larger plan on the part of the Robogdi."

"And Glyncalder?" Darius said. Glyncalder was the nearest Celtic settlement, and inhabited by the Robogdi.

"All quiet. Sir, might I make a suggestion?" Marcus didn't pause long enough for Darius to respond. "After our next capture, we should preserve the life of at least one of the elves. Attervalis's translator could—"

"There will not always be time to wait for the translator," Darius said. Alaine, the wan Britannian man who spoke the language of Hibernia in addition to Latin and his own strange tongue—the only man of such talents that the Romans had been able to scrounge up, so far—was several hours' ride away. "And in any case, these Celts rarely give up their motives, even under duress."

"Perhaps we're too kind to them," said Atticus, the hulking centurion in charge of Sylvanum's small equestrian force.

The men chuckled. Most of them. Marcus, Darius realized, looked vaguely ill, his face flushed and sweaty. Cassius and Milo, Darius's highest ranking centurions, seemed engrossed in the map on the table. Cassius leaned in to point at something, his arm brushing Milo's.

Darius swallowed his wine, thinking. "Tell me again how we came by our captives today. Don't leave out any details."

Marcus, for once, didn't leap to speak first. Instead, the fort's chronicler, a dark-eyed man of twenty named Viturian, described the Celts' capture. It struck Darius again how improbable it was, how little it fit with his knowledge of the Celts. It also struck him how close Milo and Cassius were standing together, how Cassius's hand was resting on his arm.

He turned his focus back to Viturian. The boy was too young for a rough post like this, Darius thought. And with his dark lashes and soft curls, he was also far too pretty. Darius wondered if he had let anyone into his bed, then shook himself. It wasn't the time to be distracted by such thoughts.

"Wait." He held up a hand for silence, turning back to Marcus. "Glyncalder. You said it was quiet?"

Marcus nodded. A bead of sweat stood out on his brow.

"But that's impossible." Darius set his cup down. "It's nearing their solstice celebration. The Robogdi have been gathering at Glyncalder from the smaller settlements for days."

Atticus rubbed his brow. He, too, was sweating—it was too warm in the room; the open window let in no breeze at all. "Our scouts saw little activity. All seemed abed, apart from the odd woman or child."

Darius felt the hair rise on his neck. At the same moment, Marcus let out a soft sound, sagging forward as if his stomach pained him.

"Excuse me, Commander," he murmured.

Darius nodded—Marcus's face was the colour of a dead fish. "Something you ate, Captain?"

Marcus only grimaced in reply and hurried out. Darius watched him go, puzzled. He turned to Cassius, who had served in Britannia with him and often shared his instincts. But Cassius, to his astonishment, was sliding a hand along Milo's thigh in full view of the other men.

Darius stared. "Are we keeping you?"

"Excuse me, sir." Milo's face was red. "My stomach."

"Your—"

But Milo was already out the door. Cassius, after murmuring something inaudible, trailed behind. Darius hadn't dismissed them. He turned to Scipio, expecting to see his own astonishment mirrored in his face. Instead, Scipio was gazing at him with something entirely different in his eyes.

Despite himself, Darius flushed. He had known that Scipio was attracted to him—he always knew, having been on the receiving end of more advances than he could count—but neither had openly acknowledged it. Darius had nothing against dallying with his men—at least, those he knew could remain professional afterward. But Scipio, with his round belly and broad shoulders, was not his type. He had thought Scipio guessed that too.

What was going on?

Scipio was not the only one gazing at Darius in a new way. Viturian was suddenly standing much closer to him— Viturian, with his slender build and fawn-like eyes. And Atticus, bulky and conspicuous, kept transferring his gaze from Darius to Viturian, with the disconcerting appearance of a man trying to decide which choice of meat suited his preference.

"Can I refill your wine, sir?" Viturian said, his voice soft and eager. He placed a hand over Darius's where it rested on the table.

Darius jerked his hand back, but not before his pulse gave a thrum. "I—no." What was wrong with him? Suddenly, Viturian's eyelashes were exceptionally distracting. What had they been speaking of?

"Glyncalder," Darius said. It was as if he were pushing the word past a wall. "Tell me again what our scouts saw."

Viturian's hand touched his arm. The boy's eyes were fever-bright, his lips parted. Darius drew back. In response, the boy lifted his hand to his own chest, and ran it down towards his waist in an unmistakeably seductive gesture.

"Viturian, I—this foolishness is beneath your dignity. You will comport yourself in a manner befitting…" Viturian's hand slid inside his own skirt, which was pushing out at the front.

Atticus, meanwhile, had grabbed Scipio by the shoulders and forced him to his knees. He lifted his skirt, revealing an extraordinary erection. Scipio's lips parted as if in polite surprise, and then Atticus's cock was in his mouth. Scipio moaned deep in his throat, his hands lifting to cup Atticus's buttocks. The man was already thrusting, his hand tangled in Scipio's hair, his eyes closed.

The sound of their pleasure triggered another wave of desire in Darius, even as he fought it with the twinned desperation and despair of a man battling a lion. Viturian's hands were on him now, moving over the planes of his chest through his uniform. Darius grabbed his wrists, intending to force him back. Instead, Viturian leaned in and pressed their mouths together.

It was a shock, feeling Viturian's tongue in his mouth. Darius's own tongue responded instinctively, twining itself with the younger man's, as Viturian made a soft, enticing sound of pleasure. He pressed his erection against Darius's thigh, and Darius felt himself hardening so quickly that it took his breath away. He fumbled with Viturian's clothes, again intending to catch hold of him, contain him, so that he could force him back. Instead, he found his hands loosening the belt that held up Viturian's skirt, letting it fall to the floor. Viturian removed his own tunic in one smooth motion, and stood naked before him, save for his boots. Just like Gaius, as he was taken by Evander in the corridor.

That memory brought a shudder of self-awareness back to Darius, and he realized the madness of the scene—Scipio on his knees with Atticus in his mouth, Viturian displaying his naked body to his commander with wanton lust in his eyes, and the table in that matter-of-fact briefing room, where they had gathered for countless discussions of dry strategy, spread with maps requiring their attention. But then Viturian was on his knees, lifting Darius's skirt, and then his mouth was on his cock, and Darius lost himself to the lust expanding in his body like the petals of a dark flower.

He cupped Viturian's head as the man took him. For all his youth, Viturian was no novice. His tongue swirled around him, exploring, before sliding up in the most delicious way to press itself into the head. Viturian lingered there for a moment, and a moan escaped Darius's mouth. Someone else was moaning—Atticus, he assumed, and for a moment, the sound of their separate pleasure in that small room mingled and twined together.

He came in an explosion of light and warmth, and Viturian swallowed it all. Darius was panting, breathless. Viturian rose. He had come himself, perhaps at his own hand. Yet he began to harden again as he pressed against Darius. And Darius's body, to his amazement, responded.

Darius let out a low sound. He pressed Viturian into the wall and kissed him, so fiercely their mouths bruised. He didn't care, and neither did Viturian. They were moving rhythmically against each other, and though Darius had so recently taken his pleasure, his desire had barely ebbed with his orgasm. Now it was a swell even more powerful than before, and it was drowning him. He had to have Viturian.

He had to plant himself inside him, deeper than he had ever fucked someone before.

He broke free, dragging Viturian away from the wall and turning him, wrapping his hands around his waist. Viturian responded, eyes glazed and half closed, bending over and pressing into Darius before he was even inside him. The young man was emitting an almost animal sound now, guttural and entirely involuntary. Darius found the place where he wanted to be, and thrust himself inside. Though Viturian was unprepared, he opened smoothly, the muscles relaxing, expanding, drawing Darius in as if his body were hungry for him. It was dry and rough, but Viturian made no protest.

Atticus looked up. He had finished fucking Scipio— once in the mouth, and then elsewhere, judging by Scipio's posture. The older man seemed half asleep as he sprawled against the table, as if drunk with pleasure. Atticus came forward, his eyes wide and febrile, and gripped Viturian's hair. Then he pressed his enormous cock into the young man's mouth even as Darius pounded him from behind.

They fucked him together, the three of them finding a rhythm that forced Viturian back on Darius's cock, and then forward onto Atticus's like a pendulum. Viturian was still moaning, but deep in his throat now, his mouth entirely engulfed by Atticus's cock. Darius tightened his grip on the boy's hips as he drove into him. His eyes met Atticus's, and he saw his own fierce yearning reflected there, the sight only deepening his lust; they held each other's gazes, and it was as if they, too, were inside each other's bodies.

Viturian broke first, his senses overpowered by the doubled assault on his body, his come spattering against the stone floor. Darius was next, the spasms from Viturian's orgasm overpowering his control. He came deep inside

Viturian, the force of his orgasm almost toppling him to his knees. Atticus drew himself from Viturian's mouth at his climax, spraying his seed across the boy's face.

Darius sagged against the wall. His mind had emptied of thought, of everything but his desire, which, after briefly surrendering itself, flared up again with a heat like wildfire. Viturian was drawing himself up, somewhat bandy-legged, offering himself to Atticus as he had to Darius. Atticus leaned against the table in only his tunic, breathing hard, his cock—still flushed from Viturian's attentions—beginning to swell again.

Darius strode forward. He pushed Viturian out of the way, then shoved Atticus onto his back on the table. One of the cups overturned, spilling its contents over the map of Hibernia. Darius didn't care. He wanted Atticus's cock in his mouth, the tremendous weight of it thrusting against the back of his throat. Perhaps that would dampen the fire inside him, would do what Viturian's body couldn't, and rid him of this monstrous desire.

Darius knelt, suckling the tip. Atticus moaned, and Darius sucked harder. His hand went to his own cock as he did, stroking it in time to the attention he gave to Atticus, his mouth sliding up and down the shaft. Atticus was enormous, so enormous that Darius couldn't fit all him in his mouth, though he tried, a moan vibrating in his throat that began to echo Viturian's.

Atticus grabbed him roughly by the hair, drawing Darius to his feet again before either of them could come. He bent Darius over the table, lifting his skirt. Darius drew in a sharp breath. He didn't usually receive a man's attentions; he preferred it, generally, to be the other way around. Despite this, he found himself spreading his legs for Atticus, craving the feel of him.

Darius's eyes, glazed with lust, drifted towards the maps. The spilled cup lay on its side, and before it spread a dark stain that covered the lower half of Hibernia, its coastline and Roman forts. It was the wrong colour for wine. It had a green, brackish tinge, as if overlain by a film of algae. The smell wafted to Darius's nose. It didn't smell like wine, either, but like something mossy. Something he had smelled before, in the forests of Britannia.

Nightfire.

Darius staggered backwards, dislodging Atticus from his body in mid-thrust. He felt his own shock like a slap, briefly returning him to his senses. Atticus growled his protest and reached for Darius again, but then Viturian was there, pressing his body against Atticus.

Darius reached for the pitcher of water on the table. It tipped over beneath his unsteady hands. The water, tinged with green and scented like moss, spilled across the floor.

It was in the water.

Darius breathed in and out. The sound was a rasp. Behind him, Viturian and Atticus were moaning. Scipio's voice joined them—he was not participating, but watching the scene from the floor, pleasuring himself. Darius felt the surge of desire again, and with a monumental effort, forced it back. He stumbled to the door.

Nightfire was a rare plant in Britannia, but with an infamous reputation. Some of the Celtic tribes used it as a means to commune with their gods, gods of growth and fertility and life, at their spring festival. Darius had witnessed such a "communion" himself—when boiled and drunk, nightfire brought about total abandonment and unchecked virility. But the drug was controversial even among the Celts—many tribes, those of a more civilized bent, forbade its use out of fear of its effects, which could induce a permanent state of madness if consumed in sufficient quantities. In most instances, the drug wore off after a few hours. Darius had never sampled it, having little need for aphrodisiacs and no desire to humiliate himself in front of his men.

How had the drug ended up in the senior officers' water?

Darius's addled mind struggled to form the thought. Was this some sort of dark prank, or something more sinister—mutiny, perhaps? A means to incapacitate the senior officers and take control of Sylvanum? But who were the mutineers? And how had they obtained the drug?

He had to find the highest ranking soldier, and warn him that the Sylvanum's leaders were not, at present, compos mentis. Someone else would have to take command for the night, to hunt out the perpetrators of this act of sabotage. And, ideally, set up a guard on Darius and the others, to ensure that, in their delirious state, they did not take advantage of any of the soldiers.

Darius passed Cassius and Milo, fucking in broad view on the floor of the hall, which would soon be crowded with guardsmen heading for their shifts outside. They had evidently not been able to make it to a place of privacy before the drug overcame them. Darius picked his way around their striving bodies and discarded clothing. He forced his mind to focus on his anger rather than his lust, and it worked, but barely. He was close, too close to losing control again.

Whoever had done this would pay dearly.

Darius finally made it to the door. What he saw froze him in place.

Light flickered throughout the fort, but it was not the faint, orderly light of torches. It was a lurid red, and it was everywhere. Smoke stained the night sky.

The warehouses were burning.

Darius staggered onto the lawn. He nearly tripped over a knot of soldiers sprawled across the grass, fucking. Men ground against each other, moaning and panting, amidst the fearsome play of light and shadow and smoke. Choking, Darius kept going, his mind reeling. He spied another pair coupling against the well, located near the epicentre of the fort. Not ten yards away, a storage shed had begun to go up in flames. A hail of lit arrows streaked across the sky, originating from the darkness beyond the walls of the fort. One of these arrows hit another storage shed, and flame began to gather in the roof. The couple fucking against the well did not even look up.

The water. The well.

Darius heard Scipio's voice in his mind describing the capture of the Robogdi earlier that day. *Marcus came upon them standing in a clearing, staring through the trees at our men like startled owls.* He thought of the Robogdi steadily gathering over the last few days at Glyncalder, the settlement nearest to Sylvanum, supposedly for their midsummer festival. He saw the captive Celts lined up before him, their manner quiet and docile, saw one of them, uncharacteristically graceless, stagger and fall against the well, and pause there. Long enough—yes, more than long enough to remove something, perhaps a bottle, from an unseen pocket and pour its contents into the water.

It was not a mutiny. It was an invasion.

A cry came from the forest beyond the fort's walls, ringing and terrible. The battle cry of the Robogdi. Then they were inside the fort, the burning gate toppling inwards in a blaze of sparks. The Celts' pale hair shone in the flickering light as they ran with their bows and daggers brandished.

Not every soldier had been inebriated by the drug—a small group raced to meet the Celts, swords at the ready. Darius took a step to follow them before another wave of lust almost sent him to his knees. Someone was grunting nearby—a soldier had pushed another man against the wall, and was fumbling with his cock, preparing to enter him. But it was clear this was not a willing coupling—the man about to be fucked was held in place in a headlock, and seemed to be struggling. Darius came up behind them and rammed the hilt of his sword into the attacker's head. He went to the ground, where he lay unmoving.

"Are you all right?" Darius said.

The other man—a boy who looked to be in his late teens—regarded him with wide, terrified eyes. Recognition and relief filled his face. "Commander! The fort is under attack—somehow half the men have been drugged—"

"I know." Darius winced. The boy's cock was on full display, as were his long, well-muscled legs. "Compose yourself, soldier."

The young man, flushing, pulled his skirt back up. "I was on duty on the wall, sir, when it happened—not thirty minutes ago. Men began abandoning their posts and everything was in confusion. And shortly after, our scouts rode up with news that the Robogdi were advancing through the forest, positioning themselves to surround the fort."

It was all so neat—so efficiently, brutally planned and executed, that for a moment it took Darius's breath away. He had not seen such planning from the Celts before, though he was not, like many of his men, of the belief that they were incapable of strategy. He had seen enough evidence of their cleverness in Britannia, though it expressed itself in more focused ways than the Roman intellect. The Celts were unused to war strategy, to the sort of big-picture thinking that accompanied empire-building, because it was not how they lived. They were a race whose conflicts were settled through contained skirmishes and raids on their small, tribal neighbours.

Who among them had devised such a calculated plan to overthrow an entire Roman fort, manned by over two thousand soldiers? The Robogdi king Culland, fearsome as he was, was a man known for simple brutality, not complex schemes.

Darius ran a hand through his dark hair, trying to sort through his tangled thoughts. The boy peered at him, and seemed to recoil slightly.

"Sir, are you—? Have you—?"

"No," Darius said shortly. He had no intention of adding to the boy's panic. "But the rest of the senior officers have succumbed to the drug. It's in the water—the well. Tell me, who was head of the guard when the attack began?"

"Aurianus, sir," the boy replied. "But he—the last I saw him, he was in the hall, bending over for one of the servants."

Darius's mind raced. The sounds of fighting floated toward them, along with the crackle of the flames. Even if they defeated the Robogdi streaming through the broken gate—unlikely, with so many men incapacitated by nightfire—the fort was no longer defensible. They needed reinforcements.

"Gather what men you can find still in possession of their faculties," Darius ordered. "Exit through the east gate, and make for Attervalis with all speed."

The boy nodded, his face pale. "And you, sir?"

"I will follow from the south gate, with a second force," he said. "With luck, at least a few of us will reach Commander Albinus at Attervalis."

The boy nodded again. Saluting, he vanished into the shadows.

Darius headed in the opposite direction, toward the gate where the Robogdi were clustering, their initial, chaotic invasion countered by the Roman discipline of the men who had rushed to meet them. For all the tactical brilliance of their attack, the Robogdi fought like any other Celts—with plenty of ferocity but little cohesion. Darius easily countered an attack from one blonde, screaming man, knocking his dagger aside and driving his sword into his stomach.

Darius grimaced as he drew the blade free. Despite his height and broad shoulders, he was not a natural fighter. He was competent, of course, else he could not have risen through the ranks of the army. But he had always preferred to solve problems with words and tactics rather than the edge of a blade. He knew too many men who conquered territory through fear and violence. He himself chose to negotiate with the natives of a region, to encourage them to side with Rome to gain power over their ancient enemies, to use his eloquence to convince them that the Empire offered more advantages than self-rule. It was what he had done in Britannia, to great success—it was the reason Governor Agricola valued him so highly. Darius had hoped to use the same approach with the tribes of Hibernia.

That was looking increasingly unlikely. In fact, his own ability to survive the night was looking increasingly unlikely. He passed two men, naked and fucking in the grass, oblivious to the fighting around them. Their moans summoned another wave of desire, and this time, Darius couldn't wrestle it into submission. He turned toward the men, his sword dropping from his hand, as two of the Celts appeared before him. One loosed an arrow, which embedded itself in the back of one of the naked Romans. The other thrust his dagger toward Darius's unprotected body.

Suddenly, Marcus was there, his sword colliding with the Celt's dagger, then sliding past it into the man's chest. In a single, fluid motion, Marcus withdrew the sword, spun on his heel, and drove the blade into the stomach of the second Celt. He was moving again before either of the men had fallen, shoving Darius out of the path of a flaming arrow, and knocking a second from the sky with his sword.

They stood, both breathing hard, regarding each other. Marcus was a few inches shorter than Darius, and not a prepossessing sight, his nose a little too broad for handsomeness, his hair thinning, his mouth generally held in a thin, discontented line that matched his prickly disposition. He looked older than his twenty-five years, older than Darius did at twenty-nine. Yet he fought with a grace and power that belied his drab appearance, and Darius understood for the first time why Agricola had been so impressed by him. Darius found himself rousing again.

"Control yourself, Commander," Marcus spat, holding his sword between the two of them.

"I could say the same to you," Darius returned, noting Marcus's glazed expression, the trickle of sweat on his brow. "We must make for Attervalis. We'll never retake the fort with the men in this state."

"It was in the well," Marcus said. "I don't know how, but someone drugged it."

"Not someone." Darius felt his anger rise. Usually he found it easy to master his emotions, but it seemed that nightfire reduced his willpower in more ways than one. "Those Celts you tied up and dragged back here. Did you not think to wonder why a group of Robogdi would surrender so easily to Roman captors? You opened the gates to this Trojan horse."

"The elves?" Marcus's voice held all the scorn of a spoiled patrician on his first campaign, reared on stories of Roman might and barbarian ignorance. "They're not capable of something like this."

"And yet here we stand," Darius said. "Our men incapacitated, our fort overrun by the enemy. All because a green captain with a desire to show off was outwitted by *elves*."

Marcus let out a savage sound. He tossed his sword aside and plowed into Darius, driving him into the wall. Darius, his larger size giving him the advantage in a grappling match, grabbed hold of Marcus and forced his back against the stone. Then he kissed him, hard and deep.

Marcus made a sound of protest, even as his hands lifted to slide down Darius's body. Darius pressed against him, lifting their skirts and bringing their cocks together. They were both hard, already.

Marcus groaned, twining his fingers with Darius's. His tongue slid into Darius's mouth, and it was a feeling as warm and pleasurable as that of their cocks moving against each other, their hips finding just the right rhythm. Darius sighed and gave himself over to sex, all thoughts of the battle and the Robogdi sinking from his mind as his pleasure built. His lips moved to Marcus's neck, where he lingered. Marcus slid his free hand into Darius's hair. The sounds he made now reminded Darius of Viturian. He had surrendered so abruptly that Darius wondered if he had resisted the drug until now, his desire building until it was like the weight of water pressing against a dam, ready to burst.

But as he approached the edge of his climax, Darius was suddenly shoved back, away from the warmth and pleasure of Marcus's body. He blinked, uncomprehending. Marcus was standing between him and another man—a Celt, who crumpled before Darius's eyes from the sword thrust to his stomach. Marcus must have seen the Celt approaching behind Darius, and somehow managed, in that intoxicating moment, to tear himself free of the drug's influence, retrieve his sword, and meet the Celt's attack. Darius blinked at him, stupidly amazed.

Another Celt circled them, fear and revulsion etched across his face. It was clear that he had witnessed Darius and Marcus fucking. The Celts had bizarre beliefs when it came to sex—it was the law of every tribe Darius had encountered that men could only couple with women. It was, in fact, more than a law; it was accepted as natural truth, no more debatable than the colour of the sky. Men who coupled with men, or women with women, were viewed as spirit-possessed, and slaughtered by their own kin. In Britannia, one of the tribunes had raped a Celtic boy of fifteen, a crime for which Agricola had rightly had the man whipped. But the boy had met a worse fate—after being sent back to his tribe, he had been burned alive by his own brothers, supposedly to purify the evil spirits from his body.

Darius had seen the gruesome remains with his own eyes. As a result, he had convinced Agricola to increase the penalty for rape from whipping to death as an added deterrent. The Celts' vile beliefs were not the fault of Rome, but the Empire was culpable if it did not take steps to prevent such horrors.

The Celt charged—trusting, no doubt, that his massive size would easily overcome the slight figure standing before him. Marcus watched him coolly, then dispatched him with equal coolness—a sidestep, a jab to the abdomen, then a quick, clean stroke across his neck. The Celt went down.

"Here." Marcus handed Darius his sword. His eyes narrowed. "Are you yourself?"

Darius took the sword, adjusting his skirt. "Are you?"

Marcus let out a breathy laugh. His eyes still had a glazed appearance, yet he seemed to have recovered a thin veil of composure. "Do you know how long it will be until these…effects wear off?"

"Several hours."

"Let's hope before we reach Attervalis," Marcus said. "I wouldn't want to see Commander Albinus's reaction if I shoved him against a wall."

Darius let out a chuckle, surprising himself. "You're lucky I'm the forgiving sort."

"That's an interesting word for it." Something in Marcus's eyes made Darius's thoughts return to the feeling of their bodies thrusting against each other.

"We must go," he said. "Before the Robogdi seal off all escape entirely."

Marcus nodded, tearing his eyes from Darius's. Together they turned and plunged into the night.

CHAPTER THREE

They made it out of the fort without incident, but met with a band of Celts at the edge of the forest. Marcus dispatched most of them, moving with an efficient grace that made him appear almost bored. Darius was spared the necessity of defending himself, to his relief—his desire still throbbed within him, blurring his senses. He wondered how Marcus was able to focus, but it seemed that fighting came as naturally to the man as breathing.

They had with them half a dozen soldiers—two archers, three swordsmen, and a centurion—the only men they could find still in possession of their wits. Neither Marcus nor Darius made the men aware of their own compromised states. Provided they could control themselves for the next few hours, there would be no need.

Attervalis was a journey of two or three days on foot, or half a day on horseback, via the partially constructed Roman road along the coast. It would take them longer travelling through the forest. Though Marcus scorned the idea, Darius thought it likely that the Robogdi were watching the road to Attervalis, looking to prevent any survivors from summoning reinforcements.

As they travelled through the black woods—no easy feat, for the brush was almost as dense, in places, as the shadows—swords and bows ready, Darius couldn't stop thinking of the men he had left behind. Of Cassius, who had served with him for years, oblivious to everything but his own desire. Of Scipio, his trusted ally, slouched on the floor of the briefing room as fire raged through the fort. He reminded himself that he could not help them, that he could barely help himself, but it was no comfort. He hoped the Robogdi would prize hostages over corpses once they secured the fort, but he had no idea. He didn't know the Robogdi, nor what lurked in their hearts. He didn't know Hibernia. None of them did. That truth shone even clearer after the night's events.

After they had been travelling for three or four hours, Darius called a halt beside a river of clear water. A small waterfall tumbled nearby, birthing mists that undulated like ghosts. The riverbank was rocky and broad, providing relief from the oppressive trees. They drank their fill, and Darius tried not to look as one of the men removed his tunic and splashed water over his sweaty chest.

The moon shone down, and on the treeless riverbank it felt almost bright. Darius, after running a critical eye over his soldiers, decided they would rest for a few hours to recover their strength. The men acquiesced with relief, two of them moving to build a fire on the pebbly sand. One of the archers disappeared back into the woods to scrounge up a meal. Marcus took off his tunic, going to his knees beside the river to drink. Darius turned his back. He briefly considered ordering the men to stop removing their clothing.

The woods, dense and haunted as they were, were rich with game, and the archer soon returned with three rabbits, ridiculously plump. After a hearty meal, the men seemed in better spirits, a welcome thing after what they had just witnessed.

Despite the lingering effects of the nightfire, Darius managed an approximation of his usual manner, easygoing and interested in his men's thoughts. He knew how it felt to lose battles, to feel the darkness of defeat and the loss of companions pressing against him, and he subtly encouraged his men to voice their regrets and fears. After some moments of conversation and calm reassurance, he ordered them to rest, and they obliged, their moods lightened.

Marcus had remained seated by the river, his back to the fire. Darius went to his side.

"Perhaps we could—" Marcus seemed to push the words out. "Have some privacy. Away from the men."

Darius blinked. "I thought you were able to resist the drug. You certainly seem more composed than the others."

"I can resist," Marcus said. He paused. "But around you, it is more difficult. Around you, I'd rather not fight it, for doing so becomes painful."

"Me?" Darius gazed at him. "You despise me."

Marcus chuckled. "Does it seem so? I want your position, certainly. I think you indulge some bizarre notions of chivalry in your treatment of a race of barbarians. But I couldn't despise you. You being you, your ability to command—not just to command, but to make men *want* you to command them...and looking the way you do..."

Marcus trailed off, and Darius smiled. "How do I look?"

"You know how you look." Marcus shook his head. "Do you need me to say it? Beautiful men always know they are beautiful."

Darius had received such compliments before, but not spoken in that way, with an edge of bitterness in them, by a man with downcast eyes. He examined Marcus's profile. In the moonlight, he was almost attractive—it softened his features, made them less severe.

"You don't need to say it," Darius said. Marcus chuckled.

Darius thought for a moment. Then he slid his hand into Marcus's, and led him away from the fire.

They found a flat patch of grass by the river sheltered by a boulder and a ring of trees. Darius pressed Marcus against the boulder and kissed him. The drug was beginning to wear off, and Darius's desire had lost its feverish edge. But it rose hot inside him at the feeling of Marcus's mouth against his, the brush of his tongue.

Darius fucked him slowly, taking the time to open him with his fingers and water from the river. Oil would have been preferable, but the drug still lingered in Marcus's body too, and he opened easily for Darius's cock. He went to his hands and knees as Darius fucked him, both of them naked and uncaring in the cool air. Darius bent over his back, his lips at Marcus's neck, and for the first time that night, gave himself over willingly to the drug. Soft sounds escaped Marcus's throat as they moved together, not loud enough for the men to hear, over the pulse of the river. As he approached his climax, Darius could not suppress his own cries, and their voices melted together as their bodies did, pleasure erasing the distinctions between them.

They lay beside each other after, Marcus's back against Darius's chest, in a contented, companionable silence. A second wave of desire rose, and they fucked again, harder and faster this time. It was as if the drug could sense its power waning, and sought desperately to retain its hold. But the second climax brought a deeper release, and afterwards they put their clothes back on against the cold, wrapped themselves in each others' arms, and slept.

*

Darius woke to the sound of fluttering feathers.

He opened his eyes, blinking. An owl perched on a nearby branch, its tawny wings folded against its back. It regarded Darius with perfect, imperturbable calm. Darius gazed back, uneasy. The owl's eyes were a peculiar shade of silver and far too intelligent. After a long moment, during which Darius felt every beat of his heart, the bird took flight, disappearing into the forest on silent wings.

Darius was covered in gooseflesh, and not from the cold. He shook Marcus, but the man only murmured something and slept on. It was dawn, and time for them to be moving again. Darius was similarly sluggish from the aftermath of the drug. He felt spent and heavy in a way he rarely did after sex. But at least the nightfire seemed to be gone from his system.

He went to the fire, which had burned down to embers, and shook the men. They woke more readily than Marcus had, and set about readying themselves for another long march. One gathered berries, unsatisfying nourishment for eight soldiers, but welcome nonetheless. Another disappeared into the woods to relieve himself.

He was gone for some time. Darius's trepidation, his sense of being watched by unfriendly eyes, intensified. He ordered another man to search for their missing companion.

But as that man reached the edge of the trees, he let out a choked sound, staggering back. He turned to face them, his mouth round with surprise, an arrow embedded in his chest.

Darius shouted a command that sent his men scurrying for their weapons. Then a hail of arrows was upon them, and it was all he could do to protect himself.

Darius was nowhere near as skilled as Marcus at knocking arrows from the air. He saved himself from one, but a second buried itself in his thigh, and he cried out in pain. One of his men went down with an arrow in his throat; another gave a shout as an arrow struck his shoulder. Fortunately, their attackers seemed to bore of arrows, or perhaps they were out of ammunition, for suddenly they were charging out of the forest and towards the Romans, shouting a battle cry.

It was the Robogdi. Darius knew that at once—not only by their fairness, or their distinctive cry. They were perhaps a dozen in number, and there were women among them—the Robogdi seemed to be unique among Celtic tribes in their use of women soldiers. Or perhaps it was more common in Hibernia than it was in Britannia—the Romans had only encountered a handful of tribes on the island, after all.

Darius raised his sword as blood streamed down his leg, preparing to greet the woman who charged at him, but one of the Roman archers took her down first. She fell into the river, her pale eyes open and empty, her yellow hair floating around her like waterweeds.

Another of Darius's men had fallen, a Celt's dagger buried in his side. There came a shout behind him, and Darius whirled. Marcus had joined the fray, dispatching two Celts with the same negligent ease he had displayed last night, pausing between kills to knock an arrow from the air. Catching Darius's eye, he nodded, and turned to cut down the Celt who stood at the edge the fight, launching arrows at Roman targets.

The centurion who had taken an arrow to the shoulder fought on, barely—Darius hobbled to his side to rescue him from a towering Celt brandishing what looked like an axe. He buried his sword in the Celt's stomach, but the ground was uneven, and the Celt's death throes unbalanced him. He stumbled backwards, his foot catching on a rock, and fell with the weight of the Celt on top of him.

His ankle snapped. Pain seared up his leg, and the world blackened. When his vision cleared, he was in the water, his foot bent at a strange angle—a silent agony.

The soldier he had rescued bent to help him. Then he started, confusion flitting across his face. The head of an arrow protruded from his chest. Darius choked on a cry as the soldier fell, crashing into the river beside him. Revealed behind him like a pale shadow was the man who had loosed the arrow.

Darius could only stare. The archer gazing down at him, head canted as if in abstracted thought, was perhaps in his early twenties, with a slim build. He was dressed as the others were, in a long, woven tunic of greyish blue, close-fitting trousers, and boots that extended to his knees. Yet he was as different from the others, and from any man Darius had seen, as the moon is from the sun. His tousled hair was such a luminous shade of blonde that it was almost white, several strands tumbling onto his forehead, slightly damp. He had the appearance of being bleached of colour, as if he had surfaced from the mist that swirled about them like some fell god of the river. His eyes were a silvery grey that gleamed like moonlight on water.

And he was beautiful. Painfully, mercilessly beautiful. Darius could not get past it, could not stop gazing into his face, despite knowing that he was seconds away from dying at the young man's hand. For his beauty was such an unearthly thing; it froze Darius's tongue and brought an ache to his chest. For a moment, he doubted that the young man was real. Surely any second, he would give a smile, and the mist would swallow him up, returning him to whatever celestial realm he had descended from.

But none of this occurred, and the young man continued to gaze at Darius, his lips slightly parted. He had not lowered his bow. His silver eyes, fringed with dark lashes, were narrowed. Darius could not decipher the emotions that flitted across his face—all he knew was that they were gazing at each other, and that, for some unfathomable reason, he was still alive. He felt something expand within him, a feeling he couldn't interpret. Surely it was the loss of blood muddling his thoughts. The arrow was still in his thigh.

One of the Romans charged at the archer, sword raised. The young man glanced up calmly, as if at a bird that had drifted into his field of view, and buried his arrow in the soldier's throat.

Darius felt frozen. The Celt had moved so quickly that Darius's eyes couldn't follow it. One second, the arrow had been pointed at him; the next, it had killed one of his men.

The silver-eyed Celt tossed his bow aside—he was out of arrows, it seemed—and drew a dagger to meet the next Roman soldier. The dagger, Darius saw, had the carved bone hilt and wicked point that marked the man as a Robogdi assassin—a class revered by the barbarians. Unlike their brute warriors, assassins seemed to occupy an almost spiritual place in the Robogdi villages. They were rarely sent into battle, usually chosen instead for the sort of silent, catlike ambush that had earned the Robogdi such a fearsome reputation among Agricola's legions.

Even so, Darius expected the assassin to go down — the Celts were no match for Roman discipline in the arena of hand-to-hand combat. Instead, the young man dodged the soldier's sword. Mist swirled, and somehow the assassin was behind the soldier, and his dagger was slashing across his throat.

Darius was shivering. Again, the young man had moved with preternatural speed. Marcus, having killed his target, strode to meet the silver-eyed assassin. Darius shouted a warning, which Marcus — infuriating, self-involved Marcus — ignored. Then he and the assassin were engaged in battle.

The assassin let out a sound that was almost a laugh as another impossibly quick thrust was met by Marcus's sword. He darted back, eyes shining with a wild sort of amusement. There was blood on his face that had sprayed from the last man he'd killed, which somehow only added to his fey beauty, the powerful impression he conveyed of some darker aspect of nature given breath and body. They circled each other, Marcus sizing him up. He and Darius were the only Romans left alive. Their men were dead. So were the Celts, Darius realized. Marcus had killed all but one.

"Finally, an elf who can fight," Marcus drawled after another series of parries ended in a stalemate. He still seemed calm, despite the assassin's eerie grace. "But sword against dagger does not make for a fair match." He gestured with his chin to one of the Roman swords lying on the beach. "If you wish."

The assassin's eyes darted to the sword. Amazement flitted across his face as he seemed to comprehend what Marcus was offering.

"Marcus," Darius breathed. Loss of blood made his vision swim. "What are you doing, you—"

"It's what you would do, Commander," Marcus said, giving Darius an insouciant look. The idiot still hadn't comprehended the danger he was in, and was even smiling, as at a good joke. "Even barbarians deserve honourable treatment, don't they?"

Meanwhile, the assassin had reached the sword, passing in front of Marcus with his side exposed. Marcus made no move whatsoever to take advantage of the opportunity, even flashed Darius another infuriating smile. The young man hefted the sword—it was too large for his slender build; he would have to hold it two-handed to be comfortable. He gazed at it as at some curio he had never seen before. His grip was all wrong.

Marcus gave him a moment to sort himself out, and then he attacked with lightning speed. But the assassin was no longer where he had been a second ago—he had side-stepped Marcus in a swirl of mist, appearing behind him and forcing Marcus to whirl, off-balance. Marcus drove his sword toward the assassin, who parried with a bizarre series of two-handed moves that seemed entirely improvised, yet somehow managed to be effective. Then, in a neat gesture that mirrored Marcus's own negligent ease, he knocked Marcus's sword from his hand.

"No," Darius cried.

Marcus stared at the assassin, his mouth hanging open. He seemed entirely unable to process what had happened. The assassin cocked his head, considering him. Then he shifted his grip on the sword, ramming the hilt against Marcus's head. The man went down, and lay unmoving on the riverbank.

The assassin tossed the sword aside with a slight grimace, rolling his shoulder as if the heft of the weapon had pained him. He retrieved his dagger and strode to Darius's side.

Darius tried to move backwards, to reach the sword that lay only a few paces away, but his vision briefly blackened, and the assassin was there before he knew it. The young man gripped the fabric of his tunic and dragged him out of the water, pinning him to a rock.

They were close to the falls, almost pressing against them. Darius felt the spray against the side of his face, heard the pounding of the water. The assassin was so close, the warmth and breath and weight of him, his strange eyes searching Darius's face. His unearthly beauty was even more arresting at that range—Darius was struck by a strange urge to reach out and touch that thick, flaxen hair. There were worse ways to die, part of him noted distantly. There was a leaf tangled among the blonde waves, and a puff of clover.

The assassin said something, his voice urgent, the words falling upon Darius's ears like raindrops. The Hibernian tongue was strange, even stranger than the Britannian, full of lilting vowels and raspy consonants, sharp as burrs. There was a question in his words, in his eyes. Proximity clarified his beauty as it also revealed him to be flesh and blood, not some naiad of the falls. Bluish shadows lay beneath his eyes, and beside his mouth was a small blemish. It only drew attention to the elegant bow of his lips, held in tension. Darius gazed back at him, unable to move.

Voices from above. The assassin shoved Darius to his knees. He shouted something, and the voices replied.

More Celts were there, peering down from the top of the waterfall, addressing the young man in querying tones. They could not see Darius, who was hidden from view at that angle, but they could see their silver-eyed countryman.

The young man tilted his head back and gave a reply. He held his dagger casually in his hand, pointed unambiguously at Darius's throat. It was unnecessary. Darius had no desire to speak.

After a few more exchanges, the Celts above them seemed to depart. The young man released Darius and took a step back. He regarded him as if waiting for something.

"I—" Darius drew himself to his feet. His vision darkened. How much blood had he lost? The arrow was still in his leg, but he couldn't feel it.

The assassin continued to gaze at him, his eyes wandering up and down Darius's body, his expression tense, indecipherable. Still he made no move to skewer him with the dagger with which he had so easily slain Darius's men.

Darius took a painful step forward, thinking that, for some unfathomable reason, the assassin was letting him go—some barbarian code of honour? He took another step, and then the darkness overwhelmed him, and he knew no more.

CHAPTER FOUR

Darius surfaced.

He felt hot, his body bathed in sweat. Despite this, he was shaking. He tried to open his eyes, but his vision swam; his surroundings receded, then grew close again, the distances altering too quickly. He groaned, nauseated.

He realized, in some distant part of his mind, that he was feverish. His wound was infected—or perhaps the arrow had been poisoned. He glanced down at it, intending to pull it out.

Instead he saw, through the haze of his vision, a leg swathed in pale bandages. The arrow was gone. Someone drew the blanket back over his body.

"Father," he murmured. "Father."

It could only be his father—no one else had ever cared for him when he fell ill. But why did the old farmhouse smell so strangely? Forest and sweat and some sickly herb, something that reminded him—

Britannia. He was in Britannia, serving under Governor Agricola. The raven-faced man had always treated

Darius with respect, and something verging on affection—or as close to it as a general of his stature could fairly show a soldier.

"Alert the governor of my condition," he said. "He must know that I am not fit for duty. He will be looking for me."

A hand touched his face. For a moment, Darius had the impression of a pale figure leaning over him, of silver eyes glinting in the darkness like a predator's. He thought, bizarrely, of the owl—when had he seen the owl? Yesterday? Last week? How long had he been in this dark place? The silver eyes darkened to brown, ethereal beauty dimming to a rough, unshaven mien.

Marcus. Marcus was here, it was his light touch on his lips. Darius blinked, and the apparition vanished entirely.

His mouth was forced open then, and some sort of warm liquid poured down his throat. He coughed, half-choking. The substance was vile—was this doctor trying to kill him? For it must be a doctor; his father must have sent for someone. That could only mean one thing—Darius's illness was serious.

"Water," he said.

Instead of water, more of the vile liquid was tipped into his mouth. Darius swallowed, only because the alternative was choking. This doctor was utterly incompetent. Could he not understand Latin?

"That's enough," he said, fumbling with the blanket, preparing to stand. He would alert the governor to his condition himself, and get him to send this fool away. But the man spoke, his voice slicing through the darkness, and Darius paused. The words were gibberish, but the command behind them was unmistakeable. And something about the voice was familiar. It calmed some small, fearful thing inside him.

A hand cupped his head, surprisingly gentle. A cup was lifted to Darius's mouth, and he felt cool water—thank the gods—against his lips. He drank deeply, and the cup was withdrawn. Darius sank back against his bedding, his entire body trembling. Someone drew the blankets over his chest.

"Father," he murmured again.

At some point—perhaps seconds later, or perhaps hours—he sensed that the visitor had gone, and he was alone. And he recalled that his father was dead.

*

Darius would estimate, after his fever broke, that it had consumed him for four days. During that time, his world was reduced to a dark, spinning chasm, across which shapes and sounds occasionally drifted, before being pulled down into the void.

Finally, he awoke as himself again. He was burrowed in a nest of blankets in a low cave, high enough to sit up but not stand. A river played somewhere outside, and frogs croaked. It was dark—night. Someone had been there recently—he could still feel the warmth of a hand on his face.

Darius's exhausted mind could get no further than that. Finally free of the fever, he closed his eyes and slept the first deep sleep he had known in days.

*

He woke in the morning.

At least, he thought it was morning, judging by the texture of the light. It spilled into the little cave, not quite reaching his feet.

Darius blinked. He touched his face. Had he imagined the hand he had felt there? He could sense another presence, bright and flickering, recently departed.

"Hello?"

No response, save for the wind in the trees, and the ever-present murmur of the river. He could remember that clearly enough, weaving in and out of his fever dreams. He pushed himself up on one shaking hand.

Nearby, within arm's reach, was a copper jug. Darius sniffed the contents — water. Next to the jug was a cup — both had the rough-hewn appearance of Celtic vessels. Darius poured, his arm shaking as he lifted the jug, though it was far from heavy. He downed the water, then poured a second cup, downing that too.

He sagged back into his blankets. Even the simple action of drinking had wearied him, and he closed his eyes briefly. Beside the water was a pile of folded clothing. Darius squinted.

His uniform. But if —

He gazed down at himself, and started. He was clothed in the woven grey tunic of his enemy — the Robogdi. It stopped halfway down his thighs. Beneath it, he was naked and barefoot.

His ankle throbbed. He pushed the blankets back to examine it, and was surprised to find it splinted and bound, the horrific angle corrected. He was grateful not to remember that. It was badly swollen and bruised, but that was to be expected. His leg troubled him barely at all. The arrow wound was covered in a clean bandage.

He cast about the cave. It was perhaps ten feet across, and only slightly broader in length. It didn't take him long to realize that his boots were not there.

He tried to remember the last few days. He couldn't. He clung to the fact that someone had brought him here, and that someone must be coming back. Had it been Marcus? Darius remembered seeing him, but he had been feverish, and Marcus was, in all likelihood, dead. Darius thought of the scene on the beach, his men falling before the Robogdi onslaught. He shut his eyes, wishing he could block out the memories.

A thud from outside the cave. Darius's eyes flew open. The light had changed—it was afternoon now. He had fallen asleep again.

Darius fumbled to draw himself up, and he let out a hiss of pain. His ankle throbbed at the sudden movement. He lay sprawled, half on one elbow, blankets askew, as the visitor slipped inside the cave.

Pale hair and silver eyes. The grace of a stalking cat in the body of a young man. It was the Robogdi assassin.

The Celt noted Darius's wakefulness with a slight frown and a searching gaze. He was unarmed, but that meant nothing to one who killed as easily as he drew breath.

Darius fumbled for something—anything. But there was no weapon at hand, not even a stray bit of rubble. The assassin said something in a mild tone. He reached over Darius as if he were a feature of the cave floor and lifted the jug of water. Then he slipped back outside, moving without any particular urgency.

Darius half crawled, half dragged himself to the edge of the cave, his ankle protesting every inch. He blinked in the sunlight—clouds formed a patchwork over the blue, and the light dimmed and brightened. A rock ledge lay before him, stepping down to the riverbank. Trees swayed in the breeze, alive with foreign birds.

Darius's stomach clenched. He didn't recognize this place. They could have been any distance from where Darius had camped with his men, either upstream or down. The assassin crouched over the river, refilling the jug.

"Why have you helped me?" Darius said. The assassin couldn't understand, yet he felt that, in some way, he had to register his perplexity. "Why did you bring me here?"

The assassin paid him no attention. With his dishevelled hair, strange eyes, and unconscious grace, he looked like a wild animal, one that might or might not be in a pleasant mood. He returned the full jug to the cave, then set about building a fire with the sticks and logs he had deposited on the rock.

Darius had a few words of Britannian, and knew there was some overlap between the tongues. Brokenly, he repeated his questions in that language.

The assassin gave him a sharp look, a combination of surprise and confusion, as if a fish had spoken. He paused in the act of reaching for a branch, long fingers dangling. Darius repeated himself, slowly. The assassin replied, also slowly.

Darius's brow furrowed. It was a meaningless string of gibberish, to his ears—a patter of sounds alternatingly sinuous and sharp. He tried again, cobbling together enough words to ask after the fort. The Celt stared at him blankly.

Darius felt his frustration peak. He was clearly a hostage of some sort. Were the Robogdi hoping to ransom him? There could be no other reason why he had been treated, kept alive—even washed and clothed.

Yet it was equally clear that there was nothing, in that moment, he could do about his situation. He leaned back against the rock, his head pounding, his wounded ankle an agony.

The assassin had resumed ignoring him, withdrawing a knife from some hidden fold in his cloak and applying it to one of the dead rabbits next to the fire. The cloak was of a dark, beaten leather that fit close to his body, emphasizing his sharp, dangerous lines, and was of a higher quality, it seemed, than most Celtic garments. Now that Darius could examine him closely, he could see that all the clothes he wore, from the slim boots to the thigh-length tunic, were of a higher quality, finely stitched and fitted to his proportions. Assassins were worshipped among the Robogdi; clearly their occupations were also materially profitable.

The assassin worked in silence, a pale wave falling onto his forehead as he bent over the carcass. He tossed the fur and entrails into the river, all but the heart, which, after a slight pause, he held out to Darius.

Darius stared. He had no idea what he was expected to do. The heart was unexpectedly small, a bloody, delicate thing on the Celt's pale palm, like a drowned flower. Was this some sort of threat?

The assassin smiled slightly as Darius continued to stare. Then he popped the heart into his mouth, and turned to the other rabbit. Darius tried not to grimace as he licked the blood from his lips. He shook his head when the assassin offered him the second heart.

Within moments, the assassin had the fire going, lighting it with a bit of flint drawn from a pocket, and the rabbits were bubbling in a pot dangling from a spit over the flames. Darius felt his mouth water as the smell reached him. The Celt added some unfamiliar leaves to the pot, and something that looked like a sickly, gnarled potato. Darius watched him move to the edge of the river and crouch beside it in an easy, feline posture to wash the blood from his hands. He paused there a moment, the water swirling over his fingers, as if lost in thought.

Darius's gaze lingered on his profile, the tousled waves of moonlight hair, the slender build. How old was this strange Celt—twenty? In that moment, it seemed impossible to believe that this was the man who had taken the lives of Darius's men, and was among those responsible for the destruction of Sylvanum. Though Darius thought it unlikely that the assassin had taken an active hand in the Robogdi plot. It was difficult to fathom any of the Robogdi constructing a scheme of such breathtaking malevolence, its melding of brutality and humiliation that would make Roman chroniclers for generations to come shudder over their quills. Clearly King Culland possessed hidden depths of deviousness.

As Darius continued to regard him, the assassin met his eyes.

Darius started. There was something in that gaze that struck him like the embrace of icy waters. It stirred something inside him that he could not articulate. As he had before, he felt himself frozen, transfixed. Yet this time, there was no arrow pointed at his chest. There was only the strange, silver gaze of a young man, the reflected light of the river playing across his pale skin.

The assassin rose. He came to sit before Darius, barely an arm's length away, folding his legs beneath him as gracefully as he did anything else. His eyes roved over Darius's face, then down the lines of his body. Darius had never been studied in such an open, intense way before. It would have felt rude, except that there was an artlessness about it, an almost animal absence of self-consciousness.

Darius stared back. The assassin's face seemed paler than before, as if he'd slept poorly. The blemish by his mouth was gone, his skin all milky smoothness, but the shadows remained under his eyes. He searched Darius's face as if seeking something lost. Darius was unable to comprehend that expression. The assassin had looked at him that way before, when they had first lain eyes on each other. The Celt's gaze ran over his body, fixing curiously on the scars that criss-crossed the backs of Darius's hands. Darius felt a strange urge to hide them.

Minutes passed, during which it seemed that Darius did not breathe at all. With a dreamlike slowness, as if unaware of what he was doing, the assassin reached out to touch Darius's face.

Darius flinched.

The assassin drew back as if burned. A new expression surfaced—something surprised, and uncertain, and *hurt*. For a moment, he seemed years younger, merely a boy. The emotion faded as quickly as it had appeared, replaced by a wary regard.

Darius was utterly baffled. Thrown off his guard, he felt a ridiculous urge to apologize. The assassin rose, disappearing into the forest without a backward glance.

The rabbit continued to bubble over the fire. Darius stayed where he was, partly because he hadn't the energy to move. The rock was sun-warmed and pleasant. The fever had eaten at his strength, and he felt old and frail. He knew soldiers who had died from infected battle wounds. He wondered how close he'd come. He would certainly have succumbed if he'd been left on the riverbank.

It was an uncomfortable thought. The assassin had saved his life twice now—if deciding not to kill him counted. Why? If he intended to ransom him, would he leave him alone, unrestrained? Perhaps he simply trusted that Darius didn't have the strength to flee.

And what of Sylvanum? Darius desperately needed to learn the fate of the fort—had any of the men managed to reach Attervalis and summon reinforcements? If so, perhaps they would send out search parties to locate survivors. Certainly now Agricola would declare war on the Robogdi, and send additional legions to scourge them from their forests. Everything Darius knew of Agricola told him that the general would not allow such an insult to stand.

It was some time before the assassin returned. By then, Darius had added wood to the fire and stirred the stew. The sun had fallen behind the trees, and the shadows were lengthening. Birdsong faded into quiet as the forest prepared for the arrival of night.

The assassin dropped another armful of wood by the fire. Then, moving warily, he approached Darius's side. There was something in his hand—it looked like a clump of green moss. He settled next to Darius without looking at his face, then pushed back Darius's tunic to reveal the bandaged wound. His attention was cool and impersonal, his expression once again unreadable. Darius reacted involuntarily to the assassin's hand on his skin, and forced himself to be still. The man was unlikely to kill him now, after all this. Carefully, the Celt unwrapped the bandage, revealing Darius's skin to the cooling air.

Darius drew in his breath. The wound was red and inflamed, surrounded by dark, spidery lines. The assassin removed what looked like a wad of the same green moss from the injury. Despite the wound's angry appearance, it seemed to be healing, or starting to, the edges of the hole drawing together. The Celt made a satisfied sound, and then, to Darius's astonishment, placed a portion of the fresh moss he had gathered in his mouth. After chewing for a moment, he removed it, crushed and moist with saliva, and pressed it against the wound.

It stung, but that soon faded, leaving a cooling sensation in its wake that came as a sweet relief. Darius felt himself relaxing under the Celt's ministrations, even as a part of him watched as if from a distance as the Robogdi assassin who had cut down his men treated and cleaned his wound with deft, gentle hands. The young man applied more moss, then retied the bandage.

"Thank you," Darius murmured.

The Celt met his eyes. Then he turned back to the fire.

"Where are the others?" Darius said. The assassin pressed a bowl of stew into his hand. "Your men. Have you been watching me in shifts?" Clumsily, he tried to act out what he was describing. "*Robogdi*. Others."

The Celt gave him a look of such unambiguous exasperation that Darius gave up. In any event, the smell of stewed rabbit was too distracting. Darius paused in the act of wolfing the meal, forced himself to slow down. The assassin ate while gazing abstractedly into the fire. The breeze played through his pale hair. He didn't wear it long enough to tie back, like many of the Celts, but it was looser than Darius's, who wore his in the practical, closely cropped style of all Roman soldiers.

It was impossible not to stare at him, sitting there with the wind and the firelight in his hair. It wasn't just his colouring—that was unique enough. It was the supple way he moved, the unselfconscious grace that revealed itself even in the way he sat—an easy, boneless crouch. Darius recalled the way he fought, the speed and ruthless efficiency with which he had disarmed Marcus, and a little shiver played across his skin. Darius had roamed over much of the Empire in his twelve years of service, meeting people as strange in appearance as in lifestyle. Yet the man before him seemed almost a separate species.

Darius finished his meal, which was surprisingly good, the sinewy meat tendered by the fire and the unfamiliar forest vegetables lending sweetness to the broth. He leaned his head against the rock. A few stars had appeared in the darkening sky, flickering like a reflection of the campfire in a violet pool. He felt, in that moment, strangely content. The violence of Sylvanum and its aftermath seemed an unreal dream. For the first time in days, he felt almost well—the fever beaten back, his belly full, his wound numbed to a distant throb.

He started awake at the feeling of the assassin's hand on his shoulder. The sky was black now, thickly woven with stars, and the damp air was chill. The Celt had cleaned up the remains of their supper and allowed the fire to die down, flames sinking into their embers. Now he helped Darius into his bed in the cave and pulled the blankets over him. His touch remained impersonal, though Darius sensed a tension in him as he leaned over Darius's body.

"Thank you," Darius said again. The assassin heard the question in his voice, but gave him only a brief look. The cave was small; they were very close together. The air was thick with things that could not be communicated.

After placing at Darius's side the knife he had used to clean the rabbits, the assassin disappeared into the night.

CHAPTER FIVE

Darius woke late the next morning to a grey sky. He crawled out from the cave to relieve himself, wishing he could go farther from the cave to do so, for hygienic reasons, but knowing that it was impossible. He could not stand on his ankle, and so was forced to crawl everywhere—yet even crawling was uncomfortable due to the ache in his thigh and his fever-weakened limbs. When he returned to the cave, he was sweating.

A little while later, he managed to rouse himself to retrieve the remains of the stew, which the assassin had left in the pot, covered with a stone. It was cold but still good, and Darius ate until his stomach began to protest.

He had expected the assassin to return, but the sun continued its slow march across the sky, and there was no sign of that now-familiar flaxen head. Darius found himself scanning the woods frequently, glancing up whenever there was a flicker of movement, which always turned out to be a bird. He discovered another satchel that contained the moss the Celt had used on his wound, and applied a new coat himself, chewing it first as the Celt had done. He was now certain that the injury was healing, though without stitches it would remain vulnerable to reinfection for some time. Darius inspected his ankle, which also gave him no cause for concern. Given the speed at which it seemed to be healing, he suspected that it was sprained rather than broken, which was some relief.

The assassin had left food in the cave—berries and mushrooms, as well as roots that would need to be boiled before eating. As night fell, the sky began to spit, discouraging Darius from attempting a fire, and so he ate what food he could raw. As he finished his meagre meal, it began raining in earnest, and he huddled in his blankets in the dark cave.

He was quite warm enough—the small space retained his body heat. But with the storm and the darkness outside, not to mention the precariousness of his situation, he could not sleep.

He thought of his men, cut down by the Robogdi. The brightness of the fire that had consumed Sylvanum. He had no love for the place—it was an outpost, like so many outposts Darius had served at, surrounded by dark, hostile forest. But it had been an island of safety, a piece of home. Now it was gone. That dark forest had risen up and swallowed a bastion of Roman might.

He thought of his father, and home. His olive groves in the dry sunlight. The darkness outside seemed to enter the cave and take up space in his chest, a cold, heavy thing, like the falling rain. He was alone, and helpless.

Not entirely helpless. In the darkness, Darius's hand found the knife the assassin had left him. His thoughts shifted to the image of the Celt bent over him, tending to his wound. The gleam of silver eyes in the darkness. Finally, Darius slept.

*

The next day came and went, and still the assassin did not return. It rained hard, and Darius kept to the cave.

The day after that, he knew he would have to try to walk. He had no food left, and little water. His head was beginning to ache from lack of nutrition. He hadn't yet regained his strength following the infection, and he wasn't going to, huddled in a cave by himself without sustenance. It was imperative that he regain his strength. This was not a place for those weak in body or spirit.

He had decided to assume that the assassin was not going to return. Perhaps he had determined that the efforts of tending to a Roman captive were not worth whatever ransom he hoped to receive. Or perhaps the merciful impulse had driven him to spare Darius's life had been satisfied now that he was on the mend. Darius had no idea. He didn't understand what motivated the Celt, any more than he understood what motivated some winged denizen of these enchanted forests.

What was clear was that he was going to have to fend for himself.

Fortunately, the rain had stopped sometime in the night. Darius emerged from the cave, gazing at a green world that sparkled in the sunlight as if jeweled by a god's hand. The river was engorged from the rain, frothing against the rocks. Darius hobbled to the edge of the water, not an easy feat. The cave was perched on a ledge too high above the river to reach it, and so he had to make his way down several steps in the rock to get to the bank. He soon gave up trying to stand—the rock was too uneven to traverse on one foot. And so he half-crawled, half-lowered himself down to the water's edge, rolling the water jug alongside him.

It rolled too far, at one point, tumbling over the edge of the rock and into the river, where it would have been swept away, had Darius not made a desperate grab for it. Unfortunately, the movement unbalanced him, and he lost his grip on the slippery rock. With a startled cry, he tumbled off the rock and into the water.

He landed on his side, his injured leg striking a half-submerged rock. Pain exploded, sending spikes up his back. The river wasn't deep here—sitting up, it wasn't much higher than his waist. But it was so cold it left him gasping.

He tried to haul himself back onto the bank, but getting out was much more difficult than falling in. The height of the rock, slippery with spray and green lichens, and his throbbing leg conspired against him. Darius had managed to drag himself half out, falling onto his stomach in an ungainly flop, when strong hands wrapped under his arms, and pulled him onto dry land.

A familiar voice spoke words of little sense. Darius turned and met the assassin's silver eyes. He was frowning, and on his face was a look of confusion and unaffected concern. Darius felt a surge of relief that startled him as he gazed into that pale face, but he had little time to process it, for the Celt was helping Darius to his feet, slinging his arm over his shoulders to spare his ankle from the weight of his body. Though the assassin was of average height for a Celt, he was perhaps three or four inches shorter than Darius, who was tall for a Roman. His inhuman grace compensated for the imbalance, however, and Darius found himself maneuvered over the rocks with ease.

The assassin returned him to the cave and helped him into a clean, dry tunic that he must have brought with him—Darius saw several new satchels leaning against the cave wall. Darius possessed a soldierly lack of modesty as far as nudity was concerned, but he noticed that the assassin turned his face away when he stripped. Then he was swathed in surprisingly soft blankets smelling of sheep, shivering gratefully as the feeling returned to his limbs, while the Celt spoke words in a disapproving tone. Darius had the distinct impression that he was being lectured for venturing down to the river, but what else could he have done?

He motioned to the empty satchel of food. The assassin made an exasperated sound, and pointed at one of the satchels he had brought. Darius lifted the water jug, overturning it to demonstrate its empty state. The Celt, shaking his head and muttering to himself, slipped out of the cave.

Darius sat there for several moments. He had the unnerving sense that he had just carried on an argument with someone, and been perfectly understood, despite neither speaking the other's language. But then the smell of roasting meat drove all other thoughts from his mind. Tossing the blankets aside, he crawled out of the cave.

The assassin already had the fire going, despite the absence of dry wood. Though smoking mightily, the flames looked healthy enough. Balanced over them was a stick upon which a dozen small silver fish were pierced. The assassin was also boiling water mixed with leaves—some sort of tea. After a few moments of stirring, he poured a cup and handed it to Darius.

The liquid was sour and unfamiliar, but it was hot, and Darius drank it gratefully. Soon enough, the sun would peek over the trees and illuminate the riverbank, but now the air was chilly, particularly after Darius's misadventure.

"I thought you weren't coming back," Darius said. "I don't understand why you did. Why you're doing any of this."

The Celt poured himself a cup of tea and drank deeply. The shadows under his eyes were darker today, and he moved in a way that communicated weariness. There was a cut on his cheek that looked, to Darius's eyes, like the graze of a dodged arrow. It looked recent enough to still be painful, but it had stopped bleeding.

"What happened?" Darius said.

The assassin regarded him, understanding the question in his voice but not the semantics. Darius reached out unthinkingly and touched the man's cheek with his fingertip. His skin was warm and as smooth as water.

The assassin gazed at him, and Darius realized what he had done. He pulled his hand back, feeling vaguely embarrassed, though the assassin gave no sign of discomfort at his touch. He brushed the mark and shrugged. He mimed an arrow being fired, which confirmed Darius's guess but only increased his curiosity. Who had the Robogdi been fighting in the two days since the assassin's last visit? One of the other tribes? Or had Attervalis and Undanum launched a counter-offensive, perhaps aided by an additional legion from Britannia? The uncertainty made Darius ache. He gazed into the Celt's silver eyes, knowing that the answers were there, but entirely out of reach.

"What's your name?" Darius said, so that the assassin could hear he was asking a question. He touched his chest. "Darius." He then gestured at the assassin.

The assassin nodded. He said something—it was more than one word, and flowed so smoothly that Darius couldn't catch it. The Celt read the confusion in his face. He repeated himself, more slowly.

It was so strangely accented, containing sounds not even present in Latin, that Darius understood only the first two syllables. They were strange and beautiful, like the figure before him.

"Fionn?" Darius said. He wondered if the Robogdi ever shortened their names. His concern was dispelled as a smile broke out across the assassin's face, so warm and genuine that Darius felt his heart stop.

"Fionn," the assassin agreed.

Well, then. Fionn removed the fish from the fire, and they ate them with their bare hands. They were small enough to eat uncleaned, and with the tea and the berries Fionn had brought, Darius's appetite was satisfied.

After, Fionn examined Darius's ankle and changed the bandage on his thigh. Darius didn't pay much attention to what he was doing. His eyes were on Fionn's face—the sharp line of his jaw; the waves of white hair; the long, dark lashes framing those impossibly coloured eyes.

"Darius."

The sound of his name startled him. The Celt's accent gave it an exotic aspect, the vowels softened and the *r* a gentle rumble, the Roman *r* being a sound that clearly did not exist in the Hibernian tongue. Darius realized that Fionn was offering him his cup, refilled with tea. He accepted it hastily, with murmured thanks.

After disposing of the remains of their meal, Fionn went to the river's edge to wash his hands, a task he performed slowly and meticulously. He was fastidious, for a Celt—or perhaps all the Robogdi were like this. Fionn cupped the cold water and splashed it over his face, absently trailing wet fingers across the back of his neck. The sun was heating the rock now, and the air had warmed dramatically.

Darius watched the water trickle down Fionn's pale skin. A pang of desire rose within him, hot and startling in its intensity. He felt, for one dizzying moment, as he had after consuming nightfire.

He forced his gaze away. That he was physically drawn to Fionn didn't surprise him—the assassin's beauty, while of a strange aspect that bordered on inhuman, was impossible to ignore, and Darius had never been skilled at resisting beauty, even when it came attached to an enemy. But, in this case, his very natural desire alarmed him.

Fionn was a Celt. It was likely that he couldn't comprehend the possibility of Darius harbouring this sort of feeling for him, and if he did, he would react with horror and disgust.

Darius saw the Britannian boy's burned body. He couldn't understand the hatred that would drive a man to inflict such suffering on his own brother. And yet that propensity existed somewhere, in the hearts of these Celts— irrational and preposterous, but no less real for that. He would have to guard himself carefully in Fionn's presence.

Fionn came to sit beside him on the rock, droplets still glistening on his skin. In that moment, he seemed wholly a part of that dew-starred world, as unknowable as the dark forest that framed the river. Darius, distracted despite himself by Fionn's proximity, placed his cup on a rock without watching what he was doing. The cup, poorly balanced, slipped. It tumbled towards the surging river, where it was swallowed up.

Where it should have been swallowed up. Had not Fionn been there, having moved so quickly Darius hadn't seen it, catching the cup in one hand. He placed it at Darius's side, saying something in an admonishing voice.

Darius stared. He had seen Fionn move like that before, but his vision had been obscured by river mist, and Darius had been able to half-convince himself he'd imagined it. No Roman could move like that. No Celt could, either, at least none that Darius had encountered.

"How did you do that?" The question slipped thoughtlessly from his lips.

Fionn looked at him, one eyebrow quirked. He glanced at the cup, and gave a shrug that conveyed a certain weariness, as at an eternal mystery.

What are you? Darius felt a little shiver of unease, but it was nowhere near as strong as his curiosity. At some crucial point, he had stopped fearing Fionn. That didn't mean he trusted him, but it was almost as dangerous.

He saw the assassin's arrow projecting from the chest of one of his soldiers. He thought of the cool, methodical way Fionn had cut down the Romans on the riverbank. He tried to hold onto those images, but whenever he looked at Fionn, they dispersed like fog in the morning sun. He found himself thinking instead of the assassin's head bent over Darius's injury, the fall of his hair, his unexpectedly strong arm guiding him over the rocks.

Darius recalled how Fionn had hidden him from the other Robogdi that bloody day on the riverbank. He hadn't wanted them to see that he was sparing Darius's life. And he hadn't seen any other Robogdi since Fionn had brought him here. By all appearances, the assassin was helping Darius on his own initiative.

But to what end?

It was a riddle without an answer. Darius remembered thinking that before, when Marcus had easily—

too easily—rounded up a group of Celts and brought them to Sylvanum. Only that time, there had been an answer. A deadly one.

Fionn was removing items from the satchels he had brought, organizing them in the cave upon the natural shelves formed by the rock. It was food, mostly—rough chunks of salted meat; something that looked like a large biscuit, but was likely the rock-like, inedible bread stomached by some Hibernian tribes; several apples; more leaves of the kind Fionn had brewed that morning; and a fearsome cheese covered in white mold. Darius had often noted that the preferred diet of a particular region mirrored its people—the bracing, hearty stews of the Germanic tribes; the jarring, chaotic spices of the East. Here it seemed the food was designed to pick off the weak while testing the tolerances of the strong.

After arranging things to the satisfaction of his fastidious nature, which took some time, Fionn returned to Darius's side. He pointed to the sun, then mimed it setting and rising again. Just before it set for the second time, Fionn stopped and pressed his hand to his chest, then to Darius's shoulder. He pointed to the food and the fire.

Darius understood. He would not see Fionn again until the next evening, when he would return with additional supplies. Seeing the comprehension in Darius's eyes, Fionn rose, murmuring something. Darius could not be certain it was a farewell, but it had that tone. Then Fionn was darting from rock to rock across the river, alighting noiselessly on the other side. He melted into the towering wall of green forest without even a ripple.

CHAPTER SIX

Darius's sleep that night was dreamless. He awoke late in the morning as a watery sun fought its way through thin cloud. It won, eventually, and Darius crawled to the edge of the rock, where he could enjoy the warmth while he soaked his ankle in the chill water. It hurt less today, a dull, background ache, and the arrow wound also seemed improved. The moss seemed to have completely drawn out the infection, and he did not bother reapplying the bandage, preferring to let the air and the river spray do its part to heal him.

He was already watching for Fionn as the sun reached its zenith and began its slow progress back into the trees. He ate some of the food, nearly breaking a tooth on the Celtic bread before deciding, wisely, to soak it first in tea. Fionn had brought him more than he could eat in a day. He wondered whether he should begin preparing dinner for the two of them—perhaps he could make a stew out of the salted meat and some of the greens Fionn had left him.

Darius let out a breath of laughter at the idea of preparing a meal for himself and a Robogdi assassin, as he would do for family—or a lover. And yet, Fionn had eaten with him, which was surely unnecessary, if all he sought was to keep Darius alive.

Darius wondered which of the Robogdi villages was Fionn's. Clearly there was one nearby, given that the assassin appeared to arrive at the cave on foot. The Romans had discovered several Celtic settlements along the River Viris—Robogdi, for the most part, but also one belonging to a mysterious tribe called the Volundi, whose territory stretched to the savage western sea. The Darini, Rome's allies, kept largely to the northeast coast.

The hours slipped by. As the sun retreated again behind the trees, Darius managed to start a fire from the kindling Fionn had left him, though it burned low and sullen, disliking the eternal damp of the wood. Darius eyed the trees, the river, the rocks jutting like broken bones. Roots swarmed from the forest, lunging out of the soil onto the bank. It was a world almost too vivid to bear, the sun stoking it to green flame.

Darius turned his face to the light, feeling its warmth relax something knotted inside him. He didn't know what had become of his fort. But he was alive. It was impossible, and for a single moment, it was enough.

Darius tended the fire. He laced his fingers, idly running a thumb over his scars as he scanned the forest for Fionn's approach. That was when he saw it.

A flicker of movement, a hint of pale hair. It appeared for a moment between the boughs on the opposite bank, and then disappeared almost as quickly. A second later, there came another flicker—farther up the river this time.

Darius froze. He groped for the knife he had been using to hack apart the meat. There was no time to do anything else—to hide, or douse the flames. He had been seen.

The forest was still. Darius wondered if it was possible that he had imagined what he'd seen, and knew in his bones that it was not. Though he saw nothing, he sensed eyes upon him. An owl let out a soft, warning sound somewhere behind him. The smaller birds had fallen silent.

Darius's heart beat slowly. He tried to imagine what he would look like to the Robogdi, if one were to stumble upon him. He was dressed in their clothes—a pale, woven tunic and close-fitting trousers. Fionn had even provided him with a pair of thin sandals that looked suspiciously like women's wear, but which spared him the impossible trial of pulling boots over his swollen ankle. Without his uniform, Darius did not appear obviously Roman—a small percentage of the Celts had dark hair and brown eyes, and with the lighter colouring he had inherited from his mother, he could perhaps pass as a tan Robogdi tribesman.

A pale figure appeared suddenly on the opposite bank, and Darius froze. It was an unfamiliar man, probably Robogdi, given the cut of his boots and the assassin's dagger he carried in his hand. He called to Darius, a question in his voice. Another man appeared, holding a bow. It was not pointed at Darius, but held in readiness.

Darius rose slowly to his feet. He could not, obviously, reply to the man, and so he simply stood, waiting. The man called again, and the archer raised his bow.

The two men seemed to size him up, an enigma in Robogdi clothing, with hair close-cropped in the Roman style. Then the archer seemed to blink, and let out a small sound of surprise. Darius recognized him in the same instant—he was one of the men he had fought during the invasion of Sylvanum, when he was near-delirious with nightfire. Darius had thought he had killed him.

"*Roman,*" the archer breathed, and the other man gave a shout. Then Darius was knocking an arrow from the air, and then he was turning, and fleeing into the forest at his back.

Stumbling into the forest. He tripped over the first root, jarring his ankle. Blackness exploded across his vision, and Darius fell onto his hands, scraping them bloody on the hostile forest floor. A distant part of him wondered if there was anything in this land, animate or inanimate, that didn't want him dead.

He lurched back to his feet immediately, but there was no benefit to it—he couldn't outrun two Robogdi. Darius had hobbled only another few yards before he heard voices at his back—the men had already crossed the river.

Darius's thoughts swam. The trees were dense, the forest swaddled in its dark finery. Could he use that to his advantage? He pressed himself into the hollow of a decaying tree—not simply because it was the only solution he could devise, but because his trembling ankle could no longer bear his weight. A moment later, they were upon him.

The first man passed by like a ghost, his footfalls a mere whisper against the soft earth. The second made more noise—he was large and red-haired, with that ruddy, peculiarly Celtic skin tone that Darius had always found alarming, as if its owner had been scrubbed raw with a brush. He thundered after the first, disappearing between the trees. Darius let out his breath.

Two more Celts followed. Then two more. They took no more notice of Darius than the first pair, equally convinced that he had charged headlong into the heart of the forest, rather than pausing here in the borderlands, in plain view, if any of the Celts happened to turn their heads.

Six Robogdi warriors. Of which three, Darius knew from the weapons they bore, were trained assassins.

He waited until the last footfall had faded, until the last leaf had ceased rustling. Then he stumbled on, moving deeper into the forest.

He didn't follow the path of the Robogdi, obviously. He headed north, and then east, following the course of a broad, shallow stream that fed into the river. His feet were soon soaked, but that was the least of his concerns. A stick scavenged from the forest floor formed a crude crutch, allowing him to move at a pace that could best be described as a steady walk. Even that was painful. Darius clenched his jaw as another hasty step jarred his already throbbing ankle.

Every minute that passed in that quiet forest pressed on him like a weight. Sooner or later—probably sooner—the Robogdi would double back, and Darius didn't like his odds when they did. Robogdi assassins seemingly knew every inch of their labyrinthine territory—they would almost certainly discover his trail, though he tried to use the stream to cloak it. They always seemed a step ahead of any Roman scout, and only through sheer brute numbers had an assassin ever been overcome in his own element.

Darius had no numbers. He had a knife, and a broken ankle. He recalled how effortlessly Fionn had cut down his men on the bank. He cast about for something, anything, that could provide a place to hide, as he could never hope to outrun his pursuers.

He was breathing heavily. He tried to still it, without success. There was a splash in the stream behind him, and then, before he could whirl to defend himself, a voice said, "Darius."

He turned and met Fionn's silver gaze. A curious feeling rose within him—a sense of overwhelming relief, followed by disquiet. Once again, he was unarmed and vulnerable, facing a silver-eyed stranger.

Only Fionn didn't feel like a stranger now. The assassin was out of breath, his pale face flushed. Darius had never seen him dishevelled like this—he had clearly run there, and fast. He held his bow, strung with an arrow, loosely at his side.

He said something, his voice low, an urgent melody of syllables. His gaze flicked to a nearby tree. He seemed to be gesturing for Darius to hide himself, but before Darius could take a step, one of the Robogdi assassins stepped out of the trees behind Fionn.

Darius had barely a second to wonder at it, the twisted symmetry of the two of them—both pale, though Fionn was the paler, his eyes glinting with an icy fire absent from the other Robogdi's watery blue gaze. Fionn was vivid as the moon in that dim forest, while the other Celt was the faintest of stars.

The Celt made a sound of surprise as Fionn turned to face him. He said something with a question in it, and then, to Darius's amazement, he bent his head in Fionn's direction. Fionn said nothing in response, and the man rose.

Fionn buried his arrow in the Celt's throat.

The forest echoed with breaking branches as the other Celts returned. One lunged out of the trees at Darius, with only the slightest rustle of the leaves to mark his approach. But Fionn was there, knocking the man's dagger from his hand and driving his own blade up into his rib cage in a perfectly executed kill.

In the same motion, Fionn retrieved the man's weapon and tossed it to Darius, who hadn't been expecting it. His instincts, honed by a decade of soldiering, reacted before he did, and he turned to meet the next man. But he was no master of the dirty brutality of a dagger fight, and it took several parries before he was able to land a thrust in the man's abdomen. It was poorly placed: the man would probably bleed out eventually, but he was still a threat. He pressed his hand against the wound and regarded Darius with murder in his eyes. Fionn, moving like a gust of wind, came behind Darius's opponent and slit his throat. He had already dispatched his own man, who lay choking on his own blood in the stream. Darius reeled, but the part of his mind that was a soldier before anything else kept count: three down.

The ruddy man stepped into the stream. He surveyed the bodies of his companions, two of which still twitched and gasped in the water, then turned his gaze on Fionn. He barely looked at Darius.

He asked a question, quietly, his voice a rumble of fury. Darius felt chilled by it, as if the icy stream had risen to cover him. Another Celt, his colouring almost as dark as Darius's, appeared at his side. The branches rustled—did the third man circle behind them, waiting for his chance to strike? Yet Darius felt unable to turn his head, transfixed by the bone-deep hatred in the red-haired man's gaze as he took Fionn in.

Fionn said nothing. He simply stood there, the stream plashing against his heels, his dagger held lightly in his left hand. He did everything left-handed. Perhaps that was part of what made him so difficult to fight, difficult to predict. He returned the warrior's fearsome gaze, his own expression unemotional—that of a man calculating a distance.

With a horrible scream, the red-haired Robogdi lunged at Fionn. Darius, who was used to Celtic battle cries, fell back a step in spite of himself. He recovered quickly, and spun to meet the third man, who charged from behind a tree, also screaming like a wounded beast. Darius's thoughts were still with Fionn, though—the red-haired Robogdi was enormous, easily twice Fionn's width, and Darius needed to put down this second threat quickly so that he could help Fionn. Fortunately, Darius's opponent was an ordinary warrior, and unskilled, or perhaps Darius had simply recovered his familiarity with his own training. He quickly ran the man through.

But the Celt, no doubt acting under the influence of the single-minded bloodlust that was the hallmark of his people, charged into Darius even as Darius skewered him with his dagger. Darius stumbled back, shoving the man off him with difficulty. He tripped over a stone and collided hard with a tree, which arrested his fall but knocked the wind from his lungs.

Fionn. The assassin had somehow, with improbable efficiency, dispatched the red-haired giant, who lay facedown in the stream, his blood undulating about him like curls of seaweed. The darker Robogdi had fled—Darius could hear him crashing through the forest, stealth forgotten in his headlong desire to leave Fionn behind.

Five down, one in retreat. Darius let out a breathless, disbelieving laugh. Fionn, after a piercing glance in his direction that Darius could not read at all, turned back to the trees, clearly thinking to follow the Celt.

An arrow flew towards his back, and before Darius could even draw breath to shout, it was buried between Fionn's shoulder blades.

Nothing, in the moment that followed, made sense, even when Darius looked back on it days later. Fionn whirled, and he did not seem hurt. For there was no arrow in his back, no wound—the arrow had hit the trunk of a tree, where it stuck, vibrating. Yet it had quite clearly entered Fionn's body. Darius had *seen* it.

The Robogdi man who had fired the arrow had seen it too. He stood at the edge of the stream, the whites of his eyes clearly visible even through the layered shadow of the forest. He nocked another arrow, but Fionn didn't need to bother batting it aside—it came nowhere near its target. The man pointed the bow again, but before he could get another arrow off, Fionn was before him. Disregarding the threat posed by the weapon entirely, Fionn grabbed the man's bow and pulled him forward, thrusting his dagger into his chest in the same, practiced motion he had used before. The man was dead before he withdrew his blade.

Darius was trembling. Fionn came to his side, murmuring something, his eyes searching Darius's face. He placed a hand on Darius's arm. It was wet with the Celts' blood.

"Darius?" he said, his strange accent making more of a muddle of it than usual. He was—slightly—out of breath. Darius found himself clinging to that, for some reason. Fionn's gaze swept over his body, searching for injury.

"I'm all right," Darius said. His voice was not steady.

Fionn gestured to the woods, in the direction the remaining Robogdi assassin had fled.

Darius nodded. "Go. I'm all right."

Fionn gave him another piercing look. His hand was still on Darius's arm. When he drew it back, Darius's sleeve was bloody. Then he was gone.

Darius was alone. And not alone—the bodies were there, lying sprawled in the dirt or the water. One of them was still twitching. The red-haired giant's head was cocked at an odd angle. The wound at his throat was deep, so deep it had taken his head half off. It didn't seem like the sort of injury that could be dealt with a dagger, and yet it had been.

The forest seemed to darken. The red-haired man's limbs floated in the water, stirred by the current. Some sort of primal terror rose in Darius, a dark thing he had never felt before, even on the grisliest of battlefields, momentarily overwhelming his senses. It took control of him, whispering words in his ear: *Run. Run. Run.*

The forest began to stir.

Darius pushed himself off the tree, hefting the dagger. His ankle throbbed, but he barely acknowledged it. The forest was whispering. Or so it seemed. Not *rustling*, the sound of ordinary wind, but whispering. The sound was almost the same, but not quite. In the difference, there was awareness. And something sharp, a cold malevolence.

Darius shook.

Something was moving, perhaps behind a tree. It was either behind the tree or joined to it—a creature of human proportions, but inhuman in all other respects.

It was a pale thing, its skin the colour of rock, half-coated in a fuzz that might have been moss. Branches sprouted from its spine, spiky and jagged. Darius caught a glean of gold as its eyes turned towards him, catching the light. It moved again, and Darius saw it no more.

The creature was not alone. Others were stirring amongst the boughs, surfacing from the forest as if they had been there all along. One hissed at Darius—it had stick limbs, and a pale face that seemed all gleaming emerald eyes under a shroud of white hair. It slithered towards him and away.

The branch above him gave a shiver. Darius felt sharp, grasping fingers against his scalp, and jerked away. He lifted his dagger towards the hideous creature crouched upon the bough, its sharp, unnatural frame barely causing it to sag. This creature was like a shard of moonlight, pale and gleaming, apart from the leaves sprouting from its head and the palms of its hands. Hands that were too long, limbs that bent backwards like a cat's —

Darius stumbled into the stream. He nearly tripped over one of the bodies. Another creature crouched on the chest of one of the dead men, dipping its fingers experimentally into the severed throat. It let out a low growl, its eyes — red-gold pools in a face full of teeth and jutting bones — gleaming into Darius's. The creatures circled, taking position above Darius and on every side, closing off his escape. He felt claws bite into his leg, and whirled, slashing with his knife. But the creature was already gone.

"Darius."

He turned. Fionn was coming towards him. His eyes were so bright, in that dark forest — they reflected the light as the fey creatures' did, as human eyes did not. He seemed to hiss something at one of the creatures, but Darius could not say for certain if the sound came from his mouth or theirs. Darius suppressed an urge to take a step back, but Fionn caught his arm, and then, before Darius could stop him, placed his other hand against his face.

Darius's body reacted instantly to that cool touch. He felt as if every inch of his body reoriented itself in Fionn's direction, even as his mind rang with warnings. Fionn's thumb was against his cheekbone, soft as rain.

One of the creatures darted past, stirring the boughs and leaving in its wake the sickly sweet smell of sap. Darius tensed, anticipating another attack, his eyes trying, unsuccessfully, to follow the creature's progress. Why was Fionn just standing there? But Fionn took his jaw in hand and drew Darius's gaze back to his own.

Fionn murmured something that had Darius's name at the end. Darius felt himself caught in Fionn's gaze as an insect in a web, or a fish in a frozen pool. Fionn's expression was calm and steady. His cool hand warmed against Darius's skin. Darius smelled the creatures again, heard the leaves rustle, but his gaze didn't wander from Fionn's. The forest's murmur sank to a whisper, and then all was stillness.

CHAPTER SEVEN

He couldn't stop shaking.

He sat by the fire Fionn had built back at the cave. After leading him there, Fionn had disappeared into the forest. He didn't reappear until after the sun set and the stars flickered into being like candles in a distant temple.

When he did, he was covered in blood. His pale hair was splashed with it, as well as his hands, neck, arms, legs. Fionn alighted on the rock, a horrifically red figure. Calmly, he stripped off his tunic and boots, revealing skin like moonlight. He placed his weapons by the fire, the bow and arrow, the bone dagger. Then he dove into the river.

He was awhile in surfacing. When he did, he was like some river creature, pale and sleek, undulating easily in the rapids. He turned to Darius, and the firelight flashed against his silver eyes.

He disappeared again, then resurfaced close to the rock. He glided out, dripping, his thin trousers clinging to his body. Fionn shook the water from his hair, then knelt easily beside the river. He sat there for a moment, frozen.

Was he overcome with emotion? Darius wondered. Unwell? Then his hand slashed into the water with that eerie speed, and he was gripping a fish.

Darius watched Fionn clean and gut it, which he did with sparse, habitual motions. He attempted to rise to help him, but Fionn said something in a sharp tone. The meaning was clear, even if the words were not. Darius settled back against the rock.

"At least let me gather herbs," Darius said. Fionn ignored him. He generally paid as much attention to Darius's attempts to communicate as he did the chatter of birds, but now it rankled Darius as it hadn't before. When he tried to rise, he was ordered once again to sit.

After Fionn set the fish on a spit over the fire, he went to Darius to examine him. Darius, in an ill humour now from the shock of all that had happened and the disconcerting ease with which Fionn ordered him about, suffered his attentions stiffly. Fionn cleaned the blood and dirt from his palms, then rubbed them with a bit of the same moss he had used to treat Darius's leg. He examined Darius's ankle, which was swelling again. He *tsked* when Darius winced at his touch.

"How did you survive that arrow?" Darius said. His voice was hoarse as he gazed into the assassin's sharp, pale face. Sodden and half-dressed, the water on his pale skin glinting faintly in the starlight, he looked barely human. "Why are you protecting me?"

The Celt gave him an unreadable look before turning away. Darius felt something bubble up inside him, a fury he hadn't known he was capable of.

"Do you protect me because I'm your prisoner? Because you want to petition General Agricola to make concessions in exchange for my release?" His voice grew louder as Fionn continued to ignore him. "He won't. I may have had Agricola's trust, but I am only one man. Rome will not exchange territory for my life."

Fionn added more wood to the flames. Darius felt like the wind howling at an indifferent tree.

"You killed your own people to protect me," he continued. He couldn't stop the words pouring out of him, though he knew their futility. "Why? How do you move the way you do? What are you? What were those—those things in the woods?"

He forced himself to his feet. Fionn looked up at that, and said something in a warning voice, but Darius ignored him. "I'm not staying here," he said. Dimly he was aware of how out of control he was. His words echoed off the trees.

With that, he turned and hobbled into the forest. He had no idea where he was going. His fever-ravaged body, weakened further by the events of the day, shook in protest. He needed to eat, to sleep. But he couldn't spend another moment with Fionn. The man wasn't even human, and he was all the more dangerous because Darius had no idea what he wanted from him. For all Darius knew, he was keeping him alive just to sacrifice him in some barbarian ritual. He had seen such rituals before in Britannia, men cut to pieces or bled to death while priests chanted to their gods. Hysteria turned his thoughts into a whirlwind.

"Darius." Fionn was in front of him suddenly, his hands held up in a calming gesture. Darius shoved his hands aside, and Fionn let him. He staggered on without any idea where he was going.

"Darius," Fionn repeated. This time he took Darius's hand, and Darius felt an odd shiver trace his spine. He tried to wrench free, but Fionn held on, pulling him back toward the river. Darius seized his shoulder and shoved him.

Fionn stumbled back a few steps. Darius kept going, staggering over the roots and rocks of the darkening forest floor.

He tripped over something, and fell with a thud onto a patch of moss. Then Fionn was on top of him, and he realized he hadn't tripped—Fionn had knocked his legs out from under him. Taking advantage of his larger size, Darius rolled onto him, pressing the Celt into the ground. Silver eyes winked in the shadows like coins, and Darius felt unexpected warmth bubble in his chest at the feeling of Fionn's body beneath his. Then, relying more on his feral grace than strength, Fionn hooked his leg around Darius's and flipped him onto his back.

Darius's head hit the ground hard. Fionn murmured something that might have been an apology. Darius was breathing heavily, his chest moving against Fionn's, who barely seemed to be breathing at all. He gazed down at Darius as if struck. Darius struggled, taking advantage of his distraction, and nearly escaped. With a curse, Fionn drew a knife from his sleeve.

Darius froze. Fionn growled something. There were leaves tangled in his hair, and he looked more annoyed than anything else, as if Darius were a disobedient mutt rather than a trained officer of the Roman Empire. He tilted Darius's head to one side. Then he cut off his ear.

Darius screamed. He fought, but Fionn skilfully shifted his weight and held him in place like a boulder. He hadn't actually cut off Darius's ear; he could still feel it, because Fionn was jabbing at it with the knife over and over again. What sort of evil barbarian ritual was this? Warm blood coursed down his neck and into his hair.

Darius managed to land a blow against Fionn's stomach with his knee, and the Celt's grip briefly weakened.

But then he struck Darius in the throat, and his vision darkened.

When he came back to himself, Fionn was chanting something. His hand was pressed against Darius's lips and there was a horrible taste in his mouth. Blood. Darius choked on it, the sharp tang bringing bile to his throat. Fionn had cut himself—Darius could feel the blood dripping from his hand onto his lips—and was now forcing Darius to swallow the blood.

As soon as the horrific realization came to him, he was struggling again. Clearly, Fionn was mad. Likely he had been from the very beginning, and there was no grand design behind his decision to save Darius's life—or at least, none that a sane person would understand. Fionn was muttering under his breath, trying to keep his hold on Darius, which was proving increasingly difficult, as Darius's horror gave him new strength. Finally, he managed to roll Fionn onto a rock, which jabbed into his stomach and forced his breath out.

Darius staggered to his feet, stumbling away from him. Fionn drew himself slowly to his feet, holding his stomach and breathing hard. They stared at each other.

Darius cast a glance over his shoulder, wondering how far he would get before Fionn recovered. Not far, he wagered. He again saw his men falling on the beach, Fionn darting among them like a fish undulating through a river.

"Go then, you perfect idiot," Fionn snapped. "See how far you get on that ankle before the wolves sniff you out. I warrant I'll have to rescue you from dismemberment before you make it half a mile."

The words were precisely enunciated, delivered in a lilting accent. Darius felt as if he had been knocked over the head.

"You speak Latin," he said stupidly.

Fionn laughed. The sound was as startling as the words had been, a birdlike trill. "Of course I don't speak your oafish language. By the gods, it's like listening to sheep in rutting season. Happily, you're not speaking it either at present."

He winced, still holding his stomach, and leaned against a tree. They watched each other for a long moment, Fionn warily, Darius in stunned shock.

Fionn let out another breathy laugh. "You look like you swallowed a ghost."

Darius didn't know what to make of that bizarre image. His hand went to his ear. It was still bleeding, though not as freely.

"What did you do to me?" he whispered.

Fionn gave a grim smile. "Gave you new ears."

"By cutting them off?"

"Not quite. My, you Romans are delicate. It's just a bit of blood."

"You made me—" Darius spat, trying to rid his mouth of the taste of Fionn's blood.

"It's the only way." Fionn shoved himself off the tree. He looked weary now, as if the battle with the Robogdi had at last caught up with him. Moving with less grace than usual, he walked back to the river.

Darius trailed after him, his desire for flight utterly forgotten. He felt as stunned to be conversing with this strange creature as he would with a fish. "You put a—a spell on me."

"What of it?" Fionn didn't slow. "Would you prefer to continue babbling in your own tongue? If it pleases you, feel free."

Darius's mouth opened and closed. He saw the Latin words rise in his mind—which, he now realized with a shiver of terror, he hadn't been speaking before. He had spoken another language without realizing it. He didn't know which one, but the oddly jagged words that had fallen from his mouth weren't Latin—nor did they sound Celtic.

"I don't understand," he said, the Latin comforting to his ears.

"There you go," Fionn said. They had reached the fire again, and he pulled the fish off the flames, wrinkling his nose at its blackened state. "Perhaps you should go back to shouting at me. I'm sure that will help my understanding."

"You—" Darius felt himself slide back into that other language, as if Fionn's words had drawn it out of him. "You're a witch."

"If you like," Fionn said indifferently. He tossed the burnt fish into the river. He waded out into the rushing water, then shook his head. "The run's almost over. I'd have to stand here an hour to have a chance at another. I'll find us a rabbit." He emerged, shaking the water from his sandals, then slung a satchel over his shoulder.

"Wait," Darius said. But he may as well have spoken Latin again. Fionn slipped into the forest without a backwards glance.

CHAPTER EIGHT

It was full night before Fionn returned, with a sickle moon lurking somewhere behind the trees. Darius sat in a stupor at first. Then weariness wrapped around him like a cloak, and he nearly fell over. He managed to drag himself to a pool at the edge of the river and wash the blood off himself.

His ear had stopped bleeding—not only that, but it felt almost healed. There were small raised scars along the lobe, as if the injury was months old, and no evidence of scabbing. It was far from the strangest thing that had happened that day, and Darius forced it from his mind.

He returned to the fire, shivering, and wrapped himself in one of the sheep-scented blankets. He didn't even realize he had fallen asleep until Fionn touched him on the shoulder.

"Here," he said, looking almost awkward for the first time since Darius had known him. He put a bowl in Darius's hand, steaming with a coarse rabbit stew. Darius ate hungrily, doing his best to ignore the chewy taste of organ meat that Fionn had included—Roman custom was to use only the flesh. Fionn sat cross-legged on the rock across from him, picking daintily at his own portion.

Darius set his bowl aside as soon as he had finished, though his stomach yearned for a second serving. "What did you do to me?"

Fionn took another bite. He was only half-finished his portion. "I told you."

"You gave me the ability to speak your language." Darius shivered at how easy it felt to converse in a tongue he had only known for a few moments—he barely even noticed the words spilling from his lips, though when he forced himself to focus on them, he heard a soft rush of breathy sounds entirely unlike Latin.

"Not my language. There's no spell to teach a man a human tongue. We're speaking the language of the forest." Fionn smirked. "You don't have to look at me like that. It's not going to kill you."

"How?"

"I was born with the ability to speak their tongue. I simply shared my gift with you. They told me how."

"They," Darius repeated.

Fionn didn't elaborate, but he didn't need to. Darius's mind returned to the creatures he had seen in the forest, all gleaming eyes and sharp limbs.

He rubbed his eyes with shaking fingers. So. He had been given the ability to speak with some barbarian form of dryad. Roman dryads were generally depicted as naked maidens, breathtakingly lovely. Perhaps it shouldn't surprise him so that the Hibernian variety were frightful, savage things.

"What are you?" Darius said. "Why did you save my life? Why are you helping me?" The questions poured out like a river. "Why would you kill your own people to protect me?"

Fionn gave him a long look. Then, unexpectedly, he set his bowl aside and strode to Darius.

Darius had to stop himself from flinching away. Fionn sank with an easy grace before him, so close that their folded knees were almost touching. He took Darius's chin in one hand—not gently—and pulled him forward, searching his eyes. Darius was too surprised to do anything but let it happen. After a seemingly endless moment, Fionn released him.

He leaned back, a strange look on his face. It was lost, almost childlike.

"You truly don't know me," he said. "I thought— Perhaps some sort of test—" He bit off the rest of the words. The lost look changed to one of bone-deep disappointment, and then he seemed to compose himself. He returned Darius's blank stare with a look that was newly calculating.

Darius couldn't fathom what any of it meant. Why would Fionn have thought he would know him? "If you don't want to answer my questions, I wonder why you bothered giving me the ability to speak to you," he said, anger creeping back into his voice.

"I thought it would stop you running off if I informed you that your fort has been abandoned," Fionn said.

Darius froze. "I don't believe you. Agricola has never ordered a garrison to retreat." He added, having briefly forgotten who he was speaking to, "Agricola is the commander of the Roman forces."

"I know who he is," Fionn said.

Darius didn't know how a Robogdi assassin would know Agricola's name—perhaps from the Darini? He was used to viewing the Robogdi, along with most of the Celts, as savage denizens of the forest, barely capable of communication. But of course, that was far from the truth. His head was spinning.

"Your mighty general didn't order anything," Fionn said. "The garrison is a ruin. The fire consumed everything."

It came as a heavy blow, and Darius briefly closed his eyes. "They'll rebuild."

"Do you think so?"

The question struck Darius as ominously sly, but when he searched Fionn's face, he found nothing to confirm his suspicion. He said, "Rome never retreats. Undanum and Attervalis will provide shelter to the survivors, and stand strong against the tribes until Sylvanum is rebuilt."

Fionn smirked. "Quite the fighting spirit. I don't recall much evidence of that the night your fort burned."

Darius stared at him. Then, absurdly, he felt his face grow hot. He remembered how the nightfire had felt coursing through his veins. The absurd scene in the briefing room. "You—you saw—"

"No," Fionn said, amused. "But I heard how the night…unfolded. Clever idea to drug the well, don't you think?"

Darius's anger rose. "Dozens of my men lost their lives because of that damnable nightfire. I don't expect you to sympathize, but I will ask you not to make light of the loss of my countrymen."

"There are worse ways to die, surely?" The Celt's voice was mild, his expression impossible to interpret. Darius had no idea how to respond. Was he making a joke, or delivering a barbed insult? Speaking with Fionn was like trying to pin down the wind. This new gift was turning out to be more curse than blessing.

"Why did you say they were your men?" Fionn said before Darius could get his bearings.

"Because they are," Darius said. "Or rather were. I was the commander of Sylvanum."

"Sylvanum was under the command of Darius Lucilius," Fionn said, pronouncing Darius's name completely wrong, turning the *D* into a *V* and giving the *R* a strange twist. "I was told he was killed."

"You were either misinformed, or are presently communing with a ghost."

Fionn looked thoughtful at this, though not especially surprised. Darius felt unreasonably irritated. Surely he hadn't expected the Celt to be impressed by his rank?

"You know who I am now," he said. "Am I to be permitted to know more about the Robogdi assassin who persists in saving the life of his enemy?"

"I am not Robogdi," Fionn said with some pique, as if Darius should somehow have known better. "My tribe is the Volundi. My loyalty is to King Odran, not Culland."

Darius blinked. He knew little of the Volundi. Their territory was said to be vast, stretching across central Hibernia to the western sea. Yet their land was rugged and sparsely populated, and they were not thought to be as powerful as the Robogdi or the Darini. "But you carried the blade of a Robogdi assassin."

Fionn snorted. "The dagger? Our warriors carry them too."

"It was the Robogdi who attacked our fort."

"Not the Robogdi alone. We are allies. For a time," he added in a quieter voice, as if half to himself.

Darius grimaced. That the Robogdi had allies among the other Hibernian tribes was unwelcome news. Yet it wasn't wholly surprising—the Robogdi were known for their ferocity, not strategic foresight. Perhaps the plan to overthrow Sylvanum with the aid of nightfire had been developed by the mysterious Volundi, who were rumoured to be less warlike.

He felt a surge of frustration. He needed to take this information to Commander Albinus at Attervalis. Yet the fort was far away—he doubted he could make it in his present state.

He leaned his head back against the stone, letting the feeling ebb and then flow away. He became aware that Fionn was watching him. He was not sitting as close anymore, but still too close for comfort. His silver eyes flickered with the firelight.

"You haven't answered my question," Darius said.

"You have asked so many questions. I thought Romans valued weapons over words. Which are you referring to?"

He didn't answer. He held Fionn's gaze until the other man glanced away. Was there a flush on his pale cheeks, or was it only the light of the fire?

"You—" Fionn stopped. "You remind me of someone."

His voice was quiet. Fionn didn't elaborate, and somehow Darius knew he wasn't going to, though it was hardly an answer. He returned to the fire and began brewing tea—Darius recognized the pot and the leaves by now.

"What are you?" he said, expecting the question to cause offense. But Fionn only shrugged, as if Darius had asked about the weather.

"I don't know."

"You don't—" Darius took a breath. "How can you not know what you are?"

"Do you know what you are?"

"I'm a soldier," Darius snapped.

Fionn laughed quietly, as if at a private joke. "A soldier. Of course you would be a soldier."

"You can do impossible things," Darius pointed out. "I've never seen anyone move like you. Not to mention that, by all the laws of nature, you should have an arrow buried in your back."

"You know a great deal about the laws of nature, do you?" Fionn sounded amused. "You with your overbuilt forts and endless roads, your cities that reach higher than trees."

"What do you know of our cities?" Dimly, he was aware that Fionn had drawn him away from his questions, but he felt powerless to stop it.

"I've heard stories. We trade with several tribes in what you call Britannia."

This was an unwelcome revelation. Darius wondered what else Rome's enemies in Hibernia knew about the Empire. Were they also versed in Roman battle tactics? It made some sense, though—Rome had occupied Britannia for over a century. Clearly these barbarian hinterlands were in closer contact than Rome realized.

"And what I am to you?" he said. "A prisoner? A hostage?"

"Our first conversation is to be an interrogation, is it?" Fionn said. "How strangely you Romans express gratitude."

"Gratitude?"

"As you pointed out, I've saved your life several times now."

"So that you could hold me captive? You might as well have killed me." Darius meant it.

Fionn's gaze drifted away. "I haven't decided what to do with you yet."

"And I'm to stay here until you do?"

"Do you have another option? Your fort is in ruins. The others will follow soon enough."

Darius felt cold. "What are you talking about?"

Fionn gave him a puzzled stare. "Do you think we meant to stop with Sylvanum? To let you trample us into submission as you have the Britannians, to swear fealty to your emperor, the fat tyrant who murdered his way to the throne and now thinks himself the new Augustus?"

Darius stared at him. One could hear Domitian so characterized in many a Roman tavern, but he never expected to hear such mockery from a Hibernian barbarian. Emperor Titus's murder by his brother was mere rumour — how had it made its way to this far-flung backwater?

"We'll raze them as we razed Sylvanum," Fionn said, "and kill every man within their walls."

"There are three thousand soldiers at Attervalis alone," Darius said, shocked. "Surely you can't imagine you can stand against them. They won't fall for your trickery a second time."

Fionn's smile was dark. Darius remembered how he had seemed to enjoy killing his soldiers. Darius made it his business to keep well away from men who liked killing, and to weed them out of the ranks where possible. Killing was a necessity, not an art, as any civilized man knew. It was worse seeing that same bloodlust in Fionn's eyes, who was half a feral creature of the forest.

"We'll find a way," Fionn said. "You're Romans — your arrogance is the seed of your defeat. You managed to scare the Britannian tribes into submission, and the Darini with their bottomless hunger for gold, but the Volundi will never rest until your ships are driven from our shores. At Sylvanum, we cut you down as you fucked each other senseless—it was like lopping the heads off dandelions, the men said. All because you thought us unthinking savages, incapable of strategy or foresight. So we mounted your heads upon the broken scraps of your mighty fort. Perhaps we should have done the same with your cocks, as a reminder of the limitations of Roman intellect."

Darius rose, horrified by the callous vulgarity with which Fionn spoke of the dead. What the Celts had done had been completely without honour, violating every principle of a fair fight. To brag about it as Fionn did was something else entirely. He regarded Fionn as he would a demon that had appeared in his midst. He had been mad to think him anything other than a monster.

Fionn only laughed at his expression. "I've upset your noble Roman sensibilities. Are you going to run away again?"

"Yes." Darius's mouth was dry. "I have no intention of being prisoner to one so dishonourable as you."

"You wouldn't survive an hour in these woods. You have no idea what lurks between here and Attervalis."

Surprise made him pause. "I've spent time in your forests."

"No, you haven't. A few forays with your clanking, blundering soldiers, perhaps. That's not the same as making your way alone beneath these boughs."

Darius saw a feral face full of teeth, hands with leaves budding from the palms, reaching for him. With difficulty, he kept his voice even. "You won't stop me. I'll fight you if I have to."

"Oh, you'll fight me. Did you not see what I did to your men on the beach? You're not even as competent as your soldiers. I wonder how you maintained your authority over them."

Ridiculously, Darius's face heated. He knew he was nothing compared to Fionn, but the fact that the man had noticed he was an indifferent fighter by the standards of his own people galled him. He doubted that Fionn would understand if Darius explained that it was more honourable to win men's allegiance through the strength of your words and character than your sword arm.

"The only Roman I've met who knew how to fight was that ugly fellow," Fionn continued. It took Darius a moment to realize he was referring to Marcus. "Now that he's dead, I doubt I'll see his equal again among you lumbering oafs."

The blood throbbed in Darius's ears. He hadn't had any love for Marcus before, but their last night together had reshaped his feelings. "You didn't kill him. I saw you. You spared his life."

"I didn't kill him," Fionn agreed. "But what do you think the Robogdi did when they found his body on that beach?" He laughed. "His head is probably on a stake right now, next to his fellows. Hopefully his face won't scare the crows away."

Darius struck him.

Fionn's head snapped sideways, and he stumbled back a step. But only a step. He fixed Darius with a look that was more surprised than angry. From his reaction, Darius could have been an overlarge fly that had bitten him.

Darius's anger only intensified. For the second time that evening, he turned and blindly stumbled away from the firelight. He would make for Attervalis. He would rid himself of this feral creature if it killed him. As he fled, he grabbed the knife Fionn had used to gut the rabbit. It was still sticky with blood.

Fionn seized his shoulder, and Darius struck out blindly with the knife. The Celt had to leap back to avoid the blade. He let out a sharp word in his own tongue.

Anger beat in Darius's veins. He lunged at Fionn again, who sidestepped neatly. Darius had no idea what he was doing. He had no hope of besting Fionn—he knew that, or at least part of him did. But that part of him didn't seem to be in control anymore. The surprise had left Fionn's face, and he was beginning to look annoyed. Whatever else he was, no man liked being threatened with a knife, even if he had the skill to avoid every thrust.

Darius struck out again and again, rage making him even clumsier than usual. Each time, Fionn dodged, or knocked Darius's arm aside. If Darius had been in his right mind, he would have recognized that Fionn wasn't truly sparring with him, but merely waiting until he tired himself out. Finally, though, Fionn's patience seemed to ebb. He grabbed Darius's wrist and expertly twisted it, making him drop the knife. Then he took him by the throat and shoved him against the rock.

"Stop that," he said, reminding Darius of an idle hunter giving direction to one of his over-exuberant hounds. He didn't bother to restrain Darius with his other arm, merely gripped him by the throat. His leg was between Darius's, the better to pin him against the rock. Darius, in spite of himself, found himself overly aware of the warmth of Fionn's thigh. Their chests were almost touching.

Fionn seemed oblivious. There was a small frown between his eyes as he watched Darius.

Darius slid his hand into Fionn's hair, intending to wrench his head back. The hair was astonishingly soft, like pussywillow, falling in waves that were neither straight nor curly, but something approximating the churning of foam in a river rapid. It slid through his fingers before he was able to get a good grip. When he did, he pulled, forcing Fionn's chin up. Then he rolled Fionn over so that he was pressed between Darius and the rock.

Though Fionn could have stopped him, he let Darius gain the advantage, as if curious what he would do with it. Darius pressed him harder into the rock, his hand still tangled in Fionn's impossible hair. He still wanted to hit Fionn, but now the desire to inflict pain was mixed up with something else. He reached for Fionn's fighting hand, intending to pin it to the rock.

Fionn's lips parted in a smile that was almost appreciative. He neatly twisted his wrist free, then knocked one of Darius's legs out from under him, forcing him off balance. He rolled them again so that Darius was pinned to the rock once more. Somehow, Fionn's leg ended up pressed even more firmly between Darius's. He shifted position, rubbing against him, and Darius felt himself harden.

His face heated, and he flipped Fionn over again before—he hoped—the other man noticed. He couldn't blame the involuntary reactions of his body, but the last thing he wanted was Fionn realizing that Darius was aroused by men—or rather, in Fionn's case, a thing that wore the face of a man. Whatever reason he had for keeping Darius alive, Darius wouldn't be surprised if Fionn forgot it in the face of his disgust at Roman predilections. He was a Celt, after all.

Fionn—who could certainly have ended the scuffle by now—got his own fist around a hank of Darius's hair, drawing his head down. Then he leaned in and bit him on the ear.

Darius yelped in pain. Fionn hadn't bitten him hard enough to draw blood, and Darius was more surprised than anything. Fionn bit him again, and Darius yanked his hair hard to dislodge him. He pushed Fionn hard against the rock and leaned the full weight of his body against him. He didn't know what they were doing. It certainly wasn't any sort of fighting style Darius knew.

Away. He had to get away. He gripped the neck of Fionn's tunic and slammed him into the rock, hard enough to snap his head back. Before Fionn could recover his bearings, Darius dragged him away from the rock and across the smooth granite through which the river carved its way, intending to throw him into the rushing water.

The moon had risen above the trees while they had been scuffling, and as he pulled Fionn forward, its light fell upon them both. It struck Fionn like a spark in dry kindling, illuminating his strange hair and pale skin. Darius froze. He realized, with a dreamlike wonder, that he had never seen Fionn lit by moonlight before—all of their encounters had been in daylight, or when the moon had been shrouded by trees or cloud. Fionn writhed against him like a wildcat, dislodging his hold, and Darius staggered backwards.

Something else had begun happening in the moment the moonlight touched Fionn. Feathers sprouted from his scalp, silver and chestnut and bone-white, curving backwards like a mane of hair. His ears grew sharp and tufted, and his eyes rounded, the silver spilling out into the whites. His body changed, too, his limbs and fingers lengthening, and he grew bone-thin, every inch of skin covered in a strange, pale down. His knees snapped, a sickening sound, and his legs bent backwards. Wings erupted from his back, wings shaped like an owl's but vast, at least twice as wide as he was tall.

Darius let out a broken gasp. Fionn's wings, which had the variegated pallor of birch bark, burst open. He arrested his stumble before he plunged into the river, countering the momentum of Darius's shove. His face was contorted in pain, and then his huge eyes found Darius's, filling with an emotion he couldn't interpret. It was something that could have been rage or horror or a combination of the two, mixed with what Darius could only characterize as a *wildness*, something dark and predatory and entirely inhuman.

In a motion too quick for him to follow, Fionn grabbed Darius by the throat, drawing him forward into the shadow his wings cast by the moonlight. Darius let out an involuntary cry of horror, and Fionn's lips curled in something that wasn't a smile.

Fionn twisted his fingers through Darius's hair as he had before, forcing his head back, then he kissed him hard on the mouth.

Darius struggled out of pure shock. His mouth opened in surprise, and he tasted leaf and moss and shadow, the chill at the heart of every forest midnight and the sticky sweetness of sap. He felt the brush of Fionn's tongue, soft as a caress, and then a sting of pain. Fionn had bitten his lip. He drew back with Darius's blood on his teeth, an indefinable expression on his face. Then his wings beat once and he leapt backwards, clear across the river, and disappeared into the forest darkness.

CHAPTER NINE

Darius had only a jumbled memory of what happened next. He recalled slumping to the ground in shock, then darkness as his weakened body betrayed him. He dimly recalled making his way back to the cave on hands and knees, and he must have made it, for he awoke there the following morning.

It was late, shading into afternoon. Darius felt well-rested, and though his ankle throbbed from the events of the previous day, he was able to put weight on it. Which was good, because he had many miles ahead of him.

He would not remain there another moment.

Clearly, Fionn was some sort of forest demon, perhaps akin to a gorgon or demigod beast, like the minotaur. Either way, Darius had no intention of remaining there when he returned—if he returned.

He wondered if Fionn's countrymen knew what he was. He recalled how the Robogdi had bowed to him in the forest before Fionn put an arrow in his throat. Clearly he was held in some regard by his people, likely a result of his fighting prowess. But Darius found it hard to believe they knew that he was something inhuman entirely. On the riverbank, Fionn had demonstrated eerie skill at hand-to-hand combat, but Darius now knew, after the hours they had spent together, that he had not revealed all he was capable of.

He's hiding what he is from them. Darius hadn't the faintest idea why Fionn had been so careless about hiding what he was from him.

He emptied out the largest satchel in the cave, which held some sort of root vegetable that Fionn had evidently been planning on cooking for them at some point. He felt a tiny shiver of guilt at that, but why should he feel guilty? It was clear that Fionn saw him as little more than his prisoner. Why he had kept Darius alive was a mystery, but Darius told himself that he couldn't see himself as indebted to Fionn, a man who had threatened him and killed so many of his men.

Not to mention, a man who wasn't even a man at all. He wouldn't be beholden to the wayward whims of a monster.

He stuffed the satchel with the supplies Fionn had left him—an extra tunic; a flask that he filled with water; cheese and a small loaf of the hard bread; a blanket; a short knife intended for cutting food. He left everything else.

There was no sign of Fionn when Darius scanned the river, though this brought him little comfort. He had seen how easily Fionn could appear and disappear among the shadowy boughs.

He hobbled downstream, keeping to the riverbank for as long as he could. It formed a natural beach in this part of the forest, and Darius had to clamber over only a few uneven rocks. He wanted to avoid the forest for as long as possible. Though Fionn would surely guess he had left for Attervalis, Darius didn't want him to know which route he had taken. The river would conceal his footsteps.

Unfortunately, he had only made it a few hundred yards before the beach dissolved, and the river chasm grew steep. Darius had to clamber up the bank, slipping and sliding the whole way, clinging to roots that scratched his hands and rocks that came loose when he put his weight on them. By the time he reached the top, he wished he hadn't bothered taking the river route.

He ducked into the forest, bracing himself for something—he didn't know what. But no fell creatures attacked him, nor did Fionn leap down upon him from the treetops, monstrous wings spread wide. Birds twittered their dismay at his presence, and branches rustled in the wind.

It's only a forest, Darius thought. No different, really, than his beloved olive groves, except perhaps in scale.

He closed his eyes briefly at the memory of the groves, and for a second he could almost taste their dry scent. Then the daydream faded, and he smelled the mud on his clothes, the wet mossiness of that northern forest. He set his jaw and kept going.

He walked steadily, keeping to as northerly a course as he could, judging by the position of the sun. He wasn't a terribly skilled navigator, but Attervalis was on the coast, not far from where the river emptied into the sea. If he kept within hearing range of the rushing waters, and kept walking downstream, he would reach it, though it would take at least a day.

At least a day for an uninjured man. The longer he walked, the more his ankle throbbed. Though he'd gained back some of the strength the infection had robbed from him, he was far from his old self. He was forced to sit and rest every mile or so.

In the late afternoon, as the sun began its slow descent behind the trees, Darius leaned against a stump and wiped the sweat from his brow. His body trembled lightly from the exercise. He ate some of the bread soaked in water, and felt a little better. Still, though, he was exhausted. He was beginning to wonder just how bad the infection had been—it had never taken him so long to recover from an illness. How close to death had he come? How had Fionn brought him back when he had been so far gone?

The thought of Fionn made his stomach twist. Something rustled behind him, and he started, but it must have been a bird or a small animal, for the sound faded away. Darius allowed himself to rest another moment, and then he forced himself on.

Over the next hour or two, the rustling came again. Always it was behind him, and when he turned his head, whatever it was darted deeper into the brush. And, gradually, another thing happened: the birdsong died away. It was possible that, as night approached, the birds were simply retiring to their nooks and burrows. It was possible that he had merely attracted the interest of a squirrel or forest cat, which was now trailing him in hopes of obtaining whatever scraps he might be carrying.

You have no idea what lurks between here and Attervalis.

Darius heard the words as if Fionn had spoken them in his ear. The rustling came again, but he didn't bother to look over his shoulder this time. He turned to his right and struck out for the river.

The undergrowth grew denser nearer the water, but after a few minutes of rough going during which he got himself tangled in a thorny bush, Darius emerged onto the riverbank. He was some distance downstream of the cave, and the river was gentler here, and broader. He breathed a sigh of relief at being able to see the sky again. It was evening, but darkness was still a few hours away. The summer days were longer this far north than they were in Rome.

He turned to scan the riverbank, and his gaze alighted on a cabin.

Instinctively, Darius shrank back into the trees. Any structure he might come across in this part of Hibernia would likely belong to the Robogdi. Yet the cabin, which leaned over the flowing water, looked abandoned. The roof was partly caved in, the beaten path to the door overgrown with weeds. Behind it, someone had constructed a dam and a waterwheel, effectively diverting a side channel of the river back to its parent.

When Darius pushed open the door of the cabin, he was pleasantly surprised to find an empty hearth and a low bed with a mattress of straw. There was even a table and chair where he could sit and eat a meal like a civilized person. At the back of the cabin was a flight of stairs leading to a primitive attic with a floor made of thin saplings, also empty. Despite its outward shabbiness, the cabin seemed relatively clean. No animals had found their way inside during its owner's absence.

Darius eyed the bed longingly—he hadn't been looking forward to sleeping outdoors tonight, curled up in the forest underbrush. He decided, abruptly, that he would go no farther today. He would rest here, and make for Attervalis in the morning. He was confident he could make it to the fort by the end of the next day, even if he continued at his current pace.

He washed off the sweat of the day's journey in the river, which had an entirely different sound this far downstream—more of a low susurration than a noisy babble. He spent an hour or so foraging among the trees, and managed to gather a few handfuls of strawberries and another small red berry that Fionn had brought him once. He found a patch of mushrooms, but he wasn't certain they were edible, and left them where he found them. He longed for meat, but he disliked his odds of catching anything in his tired state, so he didn't bother trying.

After a cheerless meal consisting of berries and the remainder of his bread and cheese, Darius wrapped himself in his blanket and settled onto the bed, which was musty but surprisingly comfortable. He didn't dare light a fire, but fortunately, he didn't need one, for the summer night was mild.

Darius thought of Fionn. He thought of the way he had moved, the warping of his body as the moonlight struck him. As monstrous as he had looked, he hadn't been ugly. Strange, certainly. Unearthly. But not ugly.

He remembered the sensation of Fionn's mouth against his. Why had he done that? Why did Fionn do anything?

A shiver like a fingertip traced its way down his spine. He rolled onto his side and ordered himself to sleep.

CHAPTER TEN

He awoke from a deep, dreamless sleep to the sound of footsteps.

Darius's hand went instantly to the knife he had placed by the bed. The footsteps were coming from the empty attic above his head. Yet that was impossible—the attic had been empty when he entered the cabin, and surely if someone had come through the door, passed by his bed, and gone upstairs, he would have awoken.

His hand tightened on the knife. A wan grey light leaked through the shutters of the cabin—it was morning, or close to it. The cabin looked different than it had last night—there were two chairs rather than one, and ash in the hearth that before had been clean. Someone must have been there, moving about unnoticed as he slept. But how? He was a light sleeper.

Darius's throat was dry. The stairs creaked, and a figure made its way down. She—for it was a woman's voice he heard—was singing softly in a language he now knew. Fionn's language. The language of the forest.

The woman smiled at Darius and set her lantern down on the table. Her age was impossible to guess, and she was pretty in a well-fed, red-cheeked sort of way. Her hair was a dark cascade down her back, brushing her generous hips.

"Good morning," she said calmly, and busied herself with several baskets and bowls that also hadn't been there the previous night. "I'll make you some breakfast."

Darius glimpsed a dark loaf of bread, a bowl of goose eggs, and a bundle of apples. The woman arranged some kindling in the fire and set it alight with a single strike of her flint.

"I apologize, my lady," he said at last, warily. If this woman could speak Fionn's language, he had to assume she was like him—dangerous. "I didn't mean to impose myself upon you. I assumed this place was abandoned."

"But you're my guest." She turned to him with a smile on her round face. "How could you impose upon me? Would you care for some tea?" A pot had appeared out of nowhere. She placed it over the fire.

"Thank you," Darius said, discomfited. "But I must be on my way. Though I offer my thanks for your hospitality."

He rose, gathering up his blanket. He was unnerved to find that it had been topped with a blanket of the softest fox fur, and that beneath him was another fur blanket, just as soft. How had the woman placed a blanket beneath him while he slept? The woman made no further protest, merely hummed to herself as she cracked eggs in a pan. Darius moved towards the door.

Only to find it gone.

He ran his hands over the place where the door had been, finding only smooth wall. His pulse thrummed. He turned, only to find that the door had appeared in the opposite wall. He dashed towards it, but in the second before his hands touched it, it vanished. He turned again and found it in its original place.

"What do you fear?" the woman said, still in that calm, musical voice. She turned the eggs over the fire.

Darius forced himself to say steadily, "You will release me at once."

"Well. I'll find out soon enough." She pushed a plate towards him, heaped with egg, then sawed at the loaf of bread with an enormous knife. "Dig in. The tea's almost ready."

"I will not eat with anyone who holds me captive." Darius struggled against his rising panic. "Again, my lady, I apologize for trespassing. But you will allow me to leave."

"Apologies are of no value to me. There is only one currency I accept."

Darius was beginning to wonder if the woman was mad. "What payment do you require?"

The woman poured tea into a wooden cup elaborately carved with leaves and faces. "You must eat. You will need your strength."

Darius took a step back, and did not speak until the woman met his gaze. "I will not eat with you."

"Very well." She brushed her hands against her apron and came forward. There was a smile on her rosy face, and her black eyes were full of merriment. "If you won't eat, we may as well begin."

"Begin what?" If Darius took another step back, he would hit the wall. He scanned the cabin. The windows were tightly shuttered, likely sealed in some way, but could he break through them? He looked back at the woman, who was small for a Celt, more than a head shorter than him, and fine-boned. Yet the idea of attacking a woman was repugnant. Perhaps he could seize her arms, pin them behind her without hurting her—

"Ah, ah." The woman shook a finger at him. Then she opened her mouth and spat in his face.

Darius staggered back, striking the wall. He wiped the saliva away, but when he did, the room seemed to shudder. He opened his eyes, blinking, and found he was lying on the ground.

The cabin had disappeared. All he saw was a vast darkness, from which came the sound of trees rustling. He felt a sense of weightlessness. Was he dreaming? But hadn't he already woken up?

The woman, somehow, was on top of him, one leg on either side of his hips. She was naked, her breasts above him like enormous pale fruits. Darius was naked too, he realized. He thought of struggling, but found he couldn't. It was a horrible feeling, as if he had consumed nightfire again—as if his body and his mind were no longer in league with each other. He felt a shudder as he remembered his soldiers cut down before him, lost in their own amorousness.

Like lopping the heads off dandelions.

"I see your fear," the woman murmured. Her eyes were all black, rippled like water. She looked down at Darius, and he felt as if he were sinking into her gaze. "You fear losing yourself. Going so far from who you are that you will never return."

Her voice took on a singsong quality. "You want me," she murmured, and Darius found it was true. He tried to quell the lust rising inside him, and managed, just. He removed his hands from her thighs, which they had been caressing.

"Perhaps you have a different preference?" she murmured.

Darius bit back a cry. The witch had changed—her shoulders broadened; her chest flattened.

"Ah," the witch breathed. She touched Darius's chest, then bent her head to kiss his neck. Her cheeks were rough with stubble.

Darius tried to push the creature off, but found he could not. The witch's eyes were large and black as an insect's. She had turned herself into a large man, larger than Darius, her body heavy and muscular against his.

"There," the witch murmured. "Now fear me."

Desire surged inside him. What had the witch done to him? Desperately, he tried to fight against the reactions of his body, but he couldn't. He was hardening, and his nipples were puckered and sharp. The witch grinned, then slowly rolled him over.

"I am going to enjoy you," she murmured in Darius's ear.

Darius tried to shout, but all that came out of his lips was a soft sound closer to a grunt. The witch parted his thighs, and without even an attempt at making him more comfortable, pressed into Darius.

Darius did shout at that. The witch's cock was simply too large for his body to admit. The witch hissed something under her breath, and Darius felt another surge of desire. His thighs relaxed, and the witch pressed again. This time, Darius's body opened for her. He moaned deep in his throat.

"Fear me," the witch murmured. She began to fuck Darius, drawing her enormous cock almost entirely free of his body and then slamming it inside him again.

Part of Darius knew that he shouldn't feel aroused, given his terror, but the witch had done something to him— made it feel as if he'd taken nightfire again, an even larger dose than before. Darius dug his fingers into the earth to keep himself from moving his hips in time to the witch's thrusts. He would not lose himself again. He would not. Too much had been ruined the last time he had done so. Too many men had died.

"They died because of you," the witch murmured in his ear, even as she fucked him. "You weren't strong enough. You let your lust take over you. You're doing it again."

Darius tried to block out her voice, but his grip on reality was weakening. Was he back in Sylvanum, that night the fort burned? Was it Atticus behind him, or Marcus, thrusting faster and faster into his body?

He heard screams, and the awful, quiet sound of a sword as it slides into flesh. The nothingness around him was lit with a lurid glow. Darius turned his head. Sylvanum burned beside them. He and the witch lay in the grass beside the fort, surrounded by Romans fucking in pairs or groups while pale-skinned Celts moved among them like fish among rocks. They lifted their swords and drove them into men who didn't move to defend themselves.

"No," Darius breathed. He had to help his men. He tried to shove the witch off him, but he felt his lust rise inside him again, and his hands fell back.

The witch drew Darius into her lap so that his hips were elevated and his legs wrapped around the witch's torso. Then she entered him again in one long thrust. Darius cried out from the intensity of the pleasure. The witch's hands squeezed his thighs, then moved to his cock.

No. He clamped down on the pleasure as it rose, forced it back. He wouldn't be taken like this.

"Mmm." The witch's voice changed subtly, assuming a familiar lilt, and Darius felt the hairs rise on his neck. "I see your fear. I see your desire. What a curious man you are, that they should take the same form."

He opened his eyes, and found himself gazing into Fionn's silver eyes. The witch bent down, and Fionn's voice spoke into his ear. "You want me, Darius. Let me take you."

"Fionn," Darius said. The last remnant of his self-control crumbled at the sensation of Fionn's chest brushing his. The rush of desire that overwhelmed him was stronger than nightfire—it was lightning. He tried to press himself even closer, to feel Fionn's cock plunge even deeper inside him. The witch kept thrusting, silver eyes locked on Darius, Fionn's beautiful moonlight hair spilling over her forehead. Darius drew Fionn's head down and pressed their mouths together, moaning as he felt the brush of his tongue.

"Fionn," he murmured again. Then it crashed over him, and Darius felt his body clench and release. The witch let out a laugh and thrust once more, and Darius felt her spurt deep inside his body, a warmth like liquid fire.

The witch lay down on top of him. Darius's body was still spasming with pleasure, and he felt only a deep satisfaction at the sensation of Fionn against him. The witch's hands caressed him with fingers tipped with claws.

"There, there," the witch murmured, and it seemed she was speaking through more teeth than before. She no longer sounded like Fionn, and a part of Darius started back to himself. She wasn't above Darius anymore, but somewhere nearby in the darkness.

Suddenly, the fort was gone. Darius stood outside a house, gazing in through a window. The smell of olives was everywhere, warm and heady. Vines wreathed up the house's stone façade and coiled around the terracotta tiles of the roof. Beyond the window was a large room, simply but richly furnished, and an old man lying in a bed. He was heavily draped in blankets despite the warmth of the day.

"Father," Darius cried. But Cassius gave no sign of hearing. Another man entered the room, and Darius started as he recognized himself. He watched himself sit by his father's bedside and take his hand. His father's face was a twist of pain, but it smoothed as his gaze met Darius's, his eyes full of love.

"No." It came out as a moan. The vision was wrong. Darius hadn't been there. He had been away when his father died, fighting one of the Emperor's wars in Gaul. His father had been ill for some time, but had hidden it from Darius, being proud of his son's rise in the ranks of the army and not wanting to burden him with worry. Cassius had been a poor man in his youth, born to a merchant who frittered his wife's money away. Through shrewd investing and the right political bets, Cassius had risen to become a prosperous landowner. He had respected Darius's desire to see the world, though Darius knew it had wrenched him to watch his only son march off to war again and again. Darius's mother, Cassius's sun and stars, had died when Darius was a child, and his father had never been able to bring himself to remarry. So, Cassius had died alone. Darius had ever after been haunted by visions of his death, though he hadn't been there—or, more likely, *because* he hadn't.

He watched in helpless anxiety as his doppelganger brushed the old man's forehead with his lips. The other Darius lifted his head, and grinned at him.

Darius let out a wordless cry. The false Darius's eyes were the witch's, huge and dark. He made to leap through the window, but the vines upon the house snaked over his arms and held him in place like a iron shackles.

"Father!" Darius shouted. The witch laughed, while Cassius continued to gaze at her lovingly. A blade glinted in the witch's hand.

Terror took over him, inhabiting him as completely as his lust had, and Darius fought wildly. The vines tightened their grip in response, cutting him, but he took no notice.

The witch raised the dagger, and Cassius's eyes clouded with confusion. He held a hand out, his eyes registering a total inability to comprehend. Even as the witch stabbed him once, twice, the love in his eyes never faded.

Darius screamed. But before the witch could land the killing thrust, she gave a start. She lifted her nose as if scenting the air. Her eyes fixed on something Darius couldn't see, and she let out a deep scream that chilled Darius's blood.

Darius's father vanished, along with the bed, the vines, the house. Darius landed hard on a bed of straw, feeling as if he had been spun in a dozen circles. He blinked, frantically trying to rise, to work out where he was, but a surge of nausea rocked him back.

The witch was crouched over his bed, returned to her former guise as a lovely maiden. He was in the cabin again, his body wracked with shivering. The witch was turned away from him, facing a pale figure who seemed to weave in and out of Darius's swimming vision. Her lips were pulled back in a snarl so fearsome it didn't even sound animal.

"A fair point," a familiar voice said. "But he isn't exactly from here, so holding him to the old laws is a mite unfair."

The witch snarled again.

"True," Fionn said, his tone mild. "But not every fool belongs to you, *Od Marasceape*."

She made no reply to that. She drew back a step, and Darius thought she was giving way. But then she rushed at Fionn, her comely form melting into something huge and beastly, a creature covered in dark hair that was only vaguely female in shape, with eyes the size of hands and nothing else in her face but a maw of glittering teeth.

Fionn's dagger slashed at her before Darius even realized he had unsheathed it. He leapt past her as the witch hissed. She spun to face him, grinning—there was no evidence of injury upon her body, not a drop of blood. And now Fionn was inside her house, and the door he had stood in had vanished.

"Yes, I know," Fionn said, as if she had spoken. "You have neither flesh nor bone, nothing that I can fight. But the same is not true of these four walls, is it?"

A rumble sounded outside the cabin. The witch let out a shriek. Something slammed against the wall, and a ceiling beam came crashing to the floor. Fionn seized Darius by the arm and dragged him to his feet.

"What—I don't—what have you done, you lunatic?" Darius finally sputtered.

"You go striding into a spider's web, and I'm the lunatic?" Fionn laughed in Darius's face. That was when the wall of the cabin burst apart.

A torrent of water rushed into the room. The witch screamed, but even that was subsumed by the great roar of the river. Somehow, Fionn had weakened the dam, and the river had burst through it, eagerly laying claim to its former course. Fionn dragged Darius out of the way as half the attic came crashing down upon them, wood splintering. Darius turned, thinking that they might flee through one of the windows before they were drowned or skewered, but Fionn wrenched him back around.

"Not that way," he said with exasperation. "Can you swim, insect?"

Before Darius could even open his mouth, Fionn dragged him into the rushing torrent.

CHAPTER ELEVEN

They sailed through the cabin, striking the opposite wall, which was also splintering. It broke beneath their weight, and they were pulled out of the cabin and into the froth and foam of the river.

Darius was a poor swimmer, and would have drowned within moments had Fionn not looped his arm around his chest and held him upright. Fionn, it seemed, was as buoyant as a duck, and while the waves struck Darius in the face, he was able to keep his head mostly above water. The greater danger was the rocks. Though Darius sensed that Fionn was twisting them this way and that, keeping them away from the sharpest obstacles, the rushing water made it impossible to avoid them entirely. Darius gasped as his knee struck stone forcefully enough to make him see stars. Fionn yanked him away from a fallen tree trunk before it could do similar damage to his head. Then they were rushing on, and on, whipping past steep-sided riverbanks and endless walls of greenery.

After what seemed like an age—and several hundred bruises—the river began to slow, broadening into something gentle. Fionn pulled Darius into the shallows. He tried to stand, but fell over as soon as he put weight on his injured leg. Fionn murmured something in an uncharacteristically worried tone and helped Darius to his feet again.

"I'm fine," Darius said, but his teeth were chattering so loudly he could barely get the words out. Fionn said nothing, just led him onto the riverbank and into the shelter of a grassy clearing. They could still see the river through a row of trees.

Fionn set about building a fire with his characteristic unaffected grace. To Darius's surprise, the sky was darkening. Had he spent an entire day in the witch's hut? He shuddered. Were it not for Fionn, he would still be there.

Fionn had the fire going, and Darius drew close to it gratefully. He felt as if he would never stop shivering.

"Whatever visions you experienced in that house, they weren't real," Fionn said. He was watching Darius closely. "*Od Marasceape* is an ancient darkness. But she is no seer."

Darius stared at him. To his surprise, he felt Fionn's words lift some of the heaviness that had settled inside him. Yet he doubted he would soon forget the image of his father, helpless and alone.

"What is she?" he said. "A witch?"

Fionn shrugged slightly. "Close enough, I suppose. In some of our tales, she is said to be a goddess my people long stopped worshipping, who grew bitter and resentful. In others, she is a woman the gods cursed. It makes little difference."

He set to cleaning the fish he had caught from the river in the time it had taken Darius to relieve himself behind a bush. He put the fish over the fire and retreated into the forest, returning moments later with a handful of berries, pale mushrooms, and some needle-shaped leaves, which he rubbed into the cooked fish. He handed Darius a bowl of the odd dish. He took a hesitant bite, and then another. It was astonishingly good.

Darius had been watching Fionn as he moved, noting how he kept to the shadows. The moon shone bright in a clear, starry sky.

Darius swallowed a mouthful of fish. "Is it only moonlight that brings about the—er, transformation?"

Fionn stilled. He gave Darius a long look.

"What? Surely you didn't expect me to refrain from mentioning it." Darius let out a sound that was almost a laugh. He was tired, so tired. He was in a strange land far from home, not a mile from a witch's hut, conversing with a silver-eyed demon. He forced the laughter back, fearing he would be unable to stop.

"Yes," Fionn said finally. He placed another stick on the fire. "I can sometimes resist it, particularly if the moon is waning. But you caught me off guard."

Not a common occurrence, I'd wager, Darius thought. "Do your people know?"

A shake of his head. "My sister only, and my best friend. My mother knew, of course, but she's dead. I avoid the moonlight when I can."

Darius drank his tea. "Are you like the witch? Odd marash...marasha..."

Fionn's voice was scornful. "*Od Marasceape* is a spider who feeds off fear and lust. If I was like her, we would not be sitting here making such pleasant conversation. What horrors did she show you?"

Darius looked at his feet, hoping the darkness would conceal his flush. He was more than a little disturbed by the vision of Fionn—or, more accurately, how his body had reacted to it.

"You're changing the subject," he finally managed.

"I told you before," Fionn said. "I don't know what I am."

"How can you not know?" Darius knew that he should have been terrified by the memory of what lurked behind Fionn's beautiful face, but instead he felt only an odd irritation. "Surely your people have a name for creatures like you."

Fionn let out a long breath. He looked tired and wan, more human than Darius had ever seen him. "There are many creatures who haunt our forests. Most keep away from humans. Not even my mother knows what manner of being took her that night when—" He bit off the rest of the sentence, his expression dark.

Darius was quiet for a long moment. "Your mother was taken against her will."

Fionn's gaze was fixed on the fire. "It was Spirits' Eve—the longest night of the year, when the dead walk and dark things rise from their slumbers to plague the living. He bewitched her, led her from her bed into the deepest part of the forest, playing sweet songs on his lute. She has no memory of his appearance, only of silver eyes catching the moonlight."

Darius didn't know what to say. He felt an unexpected sympathy for the strange, pale creature before him. "And yet your mother chose to bring you into the world."

"She tried to end the pregnancy more than once. Then when I was born, she found that she loved me regardless.

She told no one but her own mother, who convinced her to keep my identity secret. Her husband, the man who raised me, believes to this day that I am his son. My mother loved him with her entire being, and he never suspected her of disloyalty."

Darius eyed him. "But you are so—well. How could no one suspect anything?"

The ghost of a smile touched Fionn's lips. "I am so, indeed. But my mother had fairy blood in her veins—distant, it's true, but fairy blood sometimes manifests in strange ways that can echo through the generations. Her family is both feared and respected for this. It was enough of an explanation to mollify all but the most suspicious, and my mother's devotion to her husband took care of the rest. I of course attempt to conceal my…abilities as much as possible. My mother taught me to do so from a young age."

"Fairy blood," Darius said faintly. Stories of fairies were widespread in Britannia. They were a sort of nature spirit, he understood, lovely but amoral. He could think of no more fitting description for the man before him. "Could that be your father's race as well?"

"Perhaps." Fionn's gaze was distant. He let out a soft, unexpected laugh. "I can count on one hand the people I have spoken of these things with."

Darius looked away. The strangeness of the situation struck him at the same moment.

"I still don't understand why you saved my life," he said quietly. "Why you keep saving it again and again."

"You wouldn't understand even if I explained it to you," Fionn said. He gave Darius a strange look that seemed woven with sadness.

"That's not good enough," Darius protested.

"I'm sorry that you Romans lack patience for mysteries."

Darius opened his mouth to retort, but his negotiator's instincts, honed by long hours communing with ferocious barbarians, made him bite the words back. He said after a moment's thought, "You don't trust me. I respect that. I've given you little reason to—we're enemies, you and I. You saved my life, and I rewarded you by fleeing."

Fionn watched him with a furrowed brow. "This has nothing to do with trust."

"Doesn't it?" Darius let the words hang in the air a moment. "I've given you little reason to have faith in me, and now I sit here badgering you with questions. Given what you've done for me, you owe me nothing—it is I who owe you." He paused. "These events have not put me in the best temper. All I can do is apologize. I won't importune you further."

"You have no need to apologize."

"I have every need," Darius said. "A man—a great chieftain in Southern Gaul, past Britannia, where the sun falls on rocky soil—once told me that trust cannot be earned—it can only be rented with coin, and lost just as easily. I fear I've squandered even the opportunity to negotiate for your faith in me."

Fionn rolled his eyes. "I have met men like that. Idiots, all."

"Is there something I can offer you in return for your answers?" Darius said. "I have, as you see, nothing but the clothes you've given me…But perhaps I could offer information of a strategic nature, if that would interest you. An exchange of trust, if you will."

He had, of course, no intention of providing Fionn with the Empire's military secrets, at least not any of importance. He was pleased to see Fionn's attention catch at the word *strategic*, but then his interest was replaced by annoyance. "Darius, must I repeat myself? I don't ignore your questions out of pique. If I knew how to answer in a way you would understand…If you would only—"

He stopped. He regarded Darius with a new look in his eyes, and then, suddenly, he laughed.

"You have a silver tongue, Commander," Fionn said. "First you humble yourself before me, then you tempt me with valuable information. You had me thinking about giving you what you asked in spite of myself. I see now why your general has elevated you to a position of power, despite the feebleness of your sword arm. You're not a soldier at all, are you? You're a bard."

Darius felt a stab of frustration, but it didn't linger, as Fionn's easy amusement was infectious. "A bard who could stand fewer reminders of his physical inadequacies, perhaps."

"Does it bother you? Knowing that you have no talent for fighting."

Darius examined him, and then, finding only curiosity in Fionn's gaze, answered honestly. "Not usually. I've managed to get by well enough without it. I suppose I could get better if I worked harder, practiced more. But I don't—well, the truth is, I don't care for it." He found himself half surprised by his own words. "I've never had much respect for violence."

"Your Empire certainly does, at least according to the tribes you call Britannians," Fionn said. "Have you ever thought you took up the wrong profession? Why not sit at home writing books and giving speeches?"

Darius smiled faintly. "I wanted to see the world."

"And have you?"

Darius met the strange silver eyes glinting at him in the firelight. Again he found himself giving voice to thoughts he had barely known he possessed. "Sometimes I think I haven't even begun."

Fionn rose. "Get some sleep. Tomorrow I'm taking you back to your people."

"I—" Darius froze. "You are?"

"It seems you're incapable of making the journey yourself," Fionn said. He didn't look at Darius.

"I thought I was your prisoner."

"I won't hold you against your will." Again that strange trace of sadness.

Darius watched him settle himself against a tree like a fawn, where he had formed a makeshift bed from moss and leaves. He had never met a more confounding person in his life. Making sense of what Fionn was, who he was, his motivations and even his words, was like trying to catch moonlight in a net. It left Darius breathless and eternally frustrated. He wanted to go to Fionn's side, shake him awake.

He thought of Fionn's transformation. How he had pressed his mouth against Darius's in something that had been more of a threat than a kiss. Or had it?

Darius watched Fionn's chest rise and fall. In the interplay of shadow and embers, his pale hair took on an eerie luminescence, like will-o-the-wisps. Darius thought he could see a shadow of the creature he had become when the moonlight touched him. Part of him wanted to see that creature again, to try to make sense of it. To map the strange lines of its body.

Darius pushed the impulse aside and settled himself on the forest floor. He was going to Attervalis tomorrow. That was what mattered. He would be among men of sense again, men whose desires were simple, measurable in coins and flesh. And then?

And then, Darius resolved as he remembered the brush of the witch's claws, the burn of the nightfire in his veins, the glittering eyes of the forest sprites, then he would leave Hibernia. Good riddance to this mad green labyrinth and everything that inhabited it. He would put in for a transfer—Agricola would grant it, he knew. He would go anywhere else in the Empire, provided it was far from here. He would turn his thoughts to roadbuilding and tax collection and soldiers' drills, and then the year would pass, and he would return to his olive groves.

Darius drew a deep breath. The memory of home was so strong he could almost feel the hot, dry air on his cheeks, even in this sylvan damp. He rolled onto his side so that he was facing away from Fionn and firmly closed his eyes.

*

Fionn shook him awake at first light. He didn't speak, merely handed Darius a bowl of some sort of hot, salty potato stew.

Darius ate quickly. Even if he spent a year with Fionn he doubted he would get used to the man tending to him this way, cooking his meals and examining his wounds. It was a level of intimacy that Darius had only experienced with his father, and sharing it with Fionn was positively eerie, like being mothered by a leopard. As Fionn examined Darius's leg with light fingers, Darius tried to focus on anything other than the spill of pale hair across his forehead, the lean lines of his body. Fionn's beauty was otherworldly; it drew him in even as it frightened him away. It was possibly the most dangerous thing Darius had encountered in Hibernia.

He finished the stew, and they set out. While Darius's state of mind certainly hadn't benefited from his stay in the witch's cabin, he found his ankle improved by the bed rest. Still, they could only travel at a hobbling pace, and Darius doubted they'd reach Attervalis that day. He found that he didn't regret the delay as much as he expected. He rejoiced at the prospect of being back among civilized people, but at the same time, part of him found it impossible to accept that he would never see Fionn again.

That was the word for it—impossible. Darius couldn't imagine waking up the next day in a Roman garrison knowing that he would never see those silver eyes again, or listen to that strange lilt of a voice. Surely it was only the mystery of the man that Darius regretted leaving, like abandoning a riddle on the cusp of resolution.

Not that he was close to understanding Fionn.

The Celt walked ahead of Darius, darting over tree trunks and slipping through brush, moving as easily through the forest as a leaf borne by the wind. He was no longer trying to conceal his inhuman grace, as he had during the early days of their acquaintance. Consequently, Darius spent the better part of the morning staring at him, helplessly fascinated, no matter how many roots and branches this caused him to trip over.

Fionn seemed to find his clumsiness amusing. After one particularly spectacular fall, he backtracked and helped Darius to his feet, saying, "I have a new respect for you Romans."

Darius shot him a look, in no mood for the barb he knew was coming. "I'm glad to hear it."

"You've managed to conquer the world despite having the physical capabilities of blind squirrels," Fionn said. "You couldn't have done that without intellect."

Darius didn't know what to say to that. He settled for honesty. "That's true enough. Though you'll find we become more than squirrels on the battlefield."

"Because you use strategy," Fionn said. "Not because your men are strong. You're smaller than us—most of you, anyway. But you plan the terrain, calculate odds, organize your soldiers into neat lines according to their value like a miser sorting his coins. Among my people, your battle tactics would be considered dishonourable trickery. They would say that if you cannot win by the strength of your arm, the accuracy of your shot, the gods have forsaken you, and you deserve defeat."

Darius nodded. "Many of the barbarian tribes of the continent took a similar view. It's why they now pay tribute to Rome."

Fionn watched him, his expression unreadable. "Tell me more about Roman intellect."

Darius scarcely knew what Fionn wanted him to say, but he was used to the feeling by now. Because he could see little harm in it, he began to speak of the Empire's governing structure, its Emperor and Senate, consuls and magistrates and justices. He told Fionn of the glory days of the Republic, a time looked upon fondly by his father, though Darius himself was less inclined to that sort of nostalgia. Emperors were not infallible, yet Rome's might had grown, its prosperity spreading to lands far and wide, under their reign. Next he told Fionn of Rome's wisest minds, particularly Cicero, of whose philosophy Darius was fond.

Fionn listened without interruption. Darius found himself growing comfortable, as if speaking of Roman ways loosened something inside him. Since Fionn offered no direction, he meandered from topic to topic, offering his opinions on Cicero's stoic paradoxes and Emperor Domitian's ambitious building programs. He had no idea how much of it Fionn understood. The man asked no questions, except to ask Darius to explain words that had no equivalent in the forest language.

Darius was almost surprised when he looked up to find the sky darkening as the sun slinking below the trees. He was tired after a day spent clambering over fallen trees and slipping on moss, but he also felt more at ease than he had at any point following the attack on Sylvanum.

He tried to help Fionn gather firewood and prepare dinner, even going so far as to snatch the bundle of fish he'd caught out of his hands. Fionn let out a sharp word in his own tongue at that, which Darius ignored. He didn't need a nursemaid anymore. Besides, Fionn's attentiveness was beginning to make him feel guilty, and he didn't want to associate guilt with a man who had slaughtered his soldiers, even if it had been a fair fight. He managed to get the fire started, but he burned the fish. Fionn ate the meal Darius served without offering any commentary save for a now-familiar glitter of amusement in his eyes.

"We should reach Attervalis tomorrow," Darius said. "I should think you'll be happy to be rid of me."

Fionn only gave him another unreadable look from across the fire. Darius sighed. "You could give me something, you know."

Fionn frowned. "Give you what?"

Darius rose slowly and moved to his side. Sometimes he felt as if Fionn were some sort of wary animal he might startle away. The other man didn't show any reaction as Darius sat next to him. "Some hint as to why you saved my life," Darius said. "Why you killed a dozen Roman soldiers without pausing for breath, then nursed their commander back to health and sent him back to the Empire's embrace."

Fionn set his bowl aside. "You must leave Araiah as soon as possible."

Darius was thrown. Araiah, he knew now, was the barbarian word for Hibernia. "Why?"

Fionn let out a soft breath. "Did you not see what we did to your fort?"

Darius grimaced. He knew Fionn believed his people could defeat Rome. They had been successful at Sylvanum, it was true, but only because they'd had the advantage of surprise, not to mention whatever diabolical mind had come up with the nightfire plot. Rome wouldn't be caught off guard again. Hibernia would join the Empire, nestling among its other jewels like an emerald in a diadem, and if the tribes gave Rome much more trouble than they already had, the hammer wouldn't fall lightly. As Fionn had himself acknowledged, the Hibernians simply didn't have the tactical knowledge to stand against the Empire.

He met Fionn's eyes. An unfathomable part of him had grown attached to this mysterious creature; there was no point in denying it. He didn't want to see him harmed. "You're the one who should leave," he said. "Go back to your village, wherever it is. Convince your chief—King Odran, you called him—to surrender to Rome at the first opportunity. Your people will be treated leniently if you do not resist the Empire. That is our way."

Fionn smiled—there was a hint of the feral, winged demon in it. "Leniency. For the people who humiliated your men at Sylvanum?"

Darius grimaced. "Best to blame that on the Robogdi. Though it would create some goodwill if you handed over the man who came up with the plot."

"And how would your general deal with him?"

Darius's face darkened. "I don't know. But I'd see that it was slow."

"How vengeful of you. I like it. I thought you Romans were all cool stoicism. What would your Cicero say?"

Darius shot him a look. "I respect Cicero. I don't take his views as gospel."

"Thank the gods for that. What a dull grey mouse of a man he must have been."

"You're changing the subject again." Suddenly, he was angry. "Why can't you answer my question?"

"Because you don't know what you're asking," Fionn snapped. "You can't. You're Roman. Your mind is all straight lines and right angles. You look at me and you want to know what I am. What you want is a word you can write down in a book next to a list of measurements and calculations. You don't even—" He seemed to force himself to stop. His breath had quickened, and there was colour in his pale face. "You will leave Araiah. Your ships move between here and Britannia regularly; take the next one out. You'll be safe there."

Some part of Darius registered how easily Fionn gave orders, as if it was something he had been born to. But he was too angry to puzzle over it. "You think you can command me? I don't owe you anything. I never asked for your help, any more than I asked for your people to kill my men."

"How you dwell on that." Fionn's voice was hard. "How many of my own people have your soldiers killed since you arrived on our shores? Are you so blind to all but your own interests to think that we would welcome you and your self-serving philosophies and your fat emperor? You're like a child who tries to pick a fight with everyone on the playground and then whines when his nose is bloodied."

Darius fumbled. "What your people did was without honour. It was—"

"You should thank us. We could have burned you alive in your beds, or stricken you with a dozen poisons. Instead we let you fuck yourselves to death. Did you not enjoy it? You Romans enjoy the embrace of other men, they say. Was it not a novelty to watch your soldiers bend over for you like whores?"

Each word was spoken with cruel precision. Darius's head spun. Part of him wanted to lash out at Fionn as he had done once before, and he knew from the look in Fionn's eyes that he wanted it too. Yet through his anger he saw what Fionn was doing, and his natural instincts—to talk rather than fight; to transmute violence into negotiation; to calm waters made turbulent by anger and mistrust—reasserted themselves.

"What do you want of me?" He said it flatly, without anger or accusation, as if he were opening a negotiation over territory. Fionn flinched as if Darius had slapped him. They gazed at each other for a long moment.

"Are you cruel, that you would ask me that, or merely thick-headed?" He said it softly, his silver eyes gleaming like coins.

Darius swallowed. His heart was behaving strangely. Fionn shifted position so that his knee pressed into Darius's thigh. He felt frozen, unable to believe that Fionn meant what he thought he meant. He was a Celt. He wasn't even human.

And yet Fionn was leaning towards him, his eyes half-lidded. His pale hair gleamed golden in the firelight. He looked in that moment like any of the lovers Darius had taken in the past just before they came together—a combination of nervousness and yearning. Darius remembered the feeling of Fionn's mouth on his.

"It can't—" Darius stumbled to a stop. "It can't be this simple."

"Isn't that how you see me?" Fionn was closer now. "A simple barbarian. Isn't that how you see us all?"

Darius could feel the blood thrumming in his veins. Every inch of his skin prickled with heat. He had given in so quickly to the witch when she had worn Fionn's face, and he realized with a start he had never wanted anyone as much as the pale creature sitting beside him. He wanted to take his face in his hands, run his fingers through his strange hair and down the nape of his neck, and press their mouths together. Fionn's lips were slightly parted.

Darius hesitated.

It was a small thing, born of fear perhaps, or disbelief. By now, he was used to Fionn's unknowability, his essential otherworldliness. It seemed impossible that Darius could be certain of what he wanted, and that it could be something as human and commonplace as a kiss. It was only the slightest of movements—a slight intake of breath, a tilt of his head.

Fionn leaned back, an unreadable constellation of emotion flitting across his face. Then he reddened and stood abruptly. It was the reaction of a boy, and as incongruous with Fionn as a hiccup in the throat of a songbird.

"No," Darius said, though he didn't know what he was protesting, for he felt as much relief as regret. "Wait. I—"

Fionn strode into the darkness without a backwards

glance.

CHAPTER TWELVE

It took Darius the better part of an hour to fight his way through the forest. He wasn't even sure that he was following the path Fionn had taken—it was the only deer trail he had been able to find, but why would Fionn bother with trails? He could melt into the trees like a shadow.

In the end, though, Darius got lucky. The trail led to a glade with a stream trickling through it, and a small waterfall that rumbled over mossy rock.

Fionn sat in the middle of the glade, one leg bent beneath him and the other dangling over the stream. He'd removed his boots, as if the chill didn't touch him. The moonlight shone full upon him, and Darius took in the sharp, terrifying lines of his wings. The fine down on his arms caught the moonlight with a subtle gleam, as if he was coated with frost. Mist from the stream wreathed him like a spell. Darius had never seen a more unearthly sight, and for a moment he merely stood among the trees, staring.

Darius didn't try to muffle his footsteps as he approached, and yet Fionn didn't look up until Darius touched his shoulder. He started almost violently, and leapt to his feet. Darius understood then why Fionn hadn't heard him, despite his preternatural senses—he simply hadn't been paying attention. His face was wet with tears.

"I'm sorry." Darius caught Fionn's hand before he could retreat. He was thrown by the tears more than he cared to admit—the idea that he was capable of affecting Fionn that way was a heady thing, like foreign wine. It was so easy to forget how young Fionn was. "I didn't mean to startle you."

Fionn said nothing. Darius could see that he wanted to pull away, to run or fly from Darius's gaze. But he didn't—Darius sensed that his pride wouldn't allow it. He settled his wings, which he had opened as if to take flight, with a gentle rustle.

Darius simply stared. Fionn's feet were no longer feet, but an owl's talons, though his hands were still human, or almost, the fingers overlong and tipped with claws. The wings were a thing of beauty. They seemed to contain every hue of white, shot through with lines of copper and gold and silver. Darius wanted to touch them. His gaze rose to Fionn's face, and he found that it was little changed, save for the enormity of his silver eyes, now like twin moons. But it was still Fionn gazing out of those eyes—the stubbornness, the ferocity, the direct challenge. The pale waves of his hair were now mixed with gleaming white feathers.

Suddenly, Darius was calm. His fear ebbed like a tide, revealing a landscape of bone-deep longing coupled with something sweet that he had never felt before.

He closed the distance between them, all traces of hesitancy gone. After all, he wasn't some green boy—this was terrain he knew how to navigate, and he felt surety swell within him. For the first time in Fionn's presence,

Darius felt as if he knew what to do, as if he'd found a map that he hadn't known existed.

Darius trailed his fingers up the inner part of Fionn's arm, marvelling at the softness of the down that covered his skin. Fionn watched the path of his fingers without moving, as if Darius had placed him under a spell.

Darius let go of his hand, and Fionn didn't draw away. He traced the line of his chin with his thumb, brushing Fionn's lower lip. Still Fionn didn't draw away. He was so still that he barely breathed, and Darius found himself wondering how many people had touched Fionn when he was like this—if anyone ever had. Darius was close enough now that he could feel the heat of Fionn's body. He hooked his hand behind Fionn's neck and gently pulled him closer.

And then, as naturally as a wave drawing itself over a beach, Darius brushed their mouths together.

Fionn's lips parted. He placed his hand on Darius's chest and slowly drew it down. Darius felt as if his touch were igniting a trail of fire. He was painfully hard even from this gentle brush of lips, and Fionn's hesitant touch. He kissed Fionn again, then drew back to place a line of kisses along his throat. Fionn's skin was warm, and the down tickled his mouth.

"Darius." The word, strangely accented, was exhaled with a breath.

Darius pushed him backwards, aiming for the broad trunk of a tree. He wanted to press Fionn against it, mould their bodies together. He was trembling. He wanted to put his mouth to every inch of Fionn's body. He had to force himself to think clearly. He had no idea how far Fionn wanted him to take this—he couldn't presume anything. He let Fionn lead the kiss, to tell Darius how deep it could go.

They were in the shadows now, and Fionn jerked back. Immediately, Darius drew his hands away. But Fionn wasn't reacting to the kiss—he was changing.

His wings shrank and folded into his back with a disconcerting series of cracks. Fionn gave a muffled gasp. Being so close, Darius could see how the wings seemed to melt through the fabric of his tunic and into his skin. The down dissolved, and the talons receded. Worst of all were his legs—they snapped at the knees with a sound that made Darius recoil. Fionn couldn't suppress a cry at that. He staggered and might have fallen if Darius hadn't caught him. Darius held him in his arms as the change rippled through him. Finally, it stopped, and Fionn stood trembling in his arms in his human guise.

"It hurts you," Darius murmured. "Doesn't it?"

Fionn lifted his head, rubbing his face with a shaking hand. He gave Darius a weary look, his silver eyes returned to their ordinary size, though they seemed to Darius even more otherworldly than they had been before.

Darius trailed his fingers up his arm. He brushed his hand through Fionn's hair gently, as if he was stroking a nervous cat. Fionn let out a soft sigh. He twined his arms around Darius's neck and kissed him.

The kiss was fiercer this time, and something deep inside Darius shivered at the brush of Fionn's tongue. He pushed the other man against the tree and pressed their bodies together as he had desired, which sent a spike of heat through his limbs. His desire was unambiguous; he knew Fionn could feel it.

Fionn leaned his head back, his eyes opening. He regarded Darius for a long moment without speaking. His eyes were shadowed, and once again, Darius could not read him, apart from the flush in his cheeks. They were still wrapped in each other's arms, breathing each other's breath.

"Is this…how you want it?" Darius said. "Tell me what you want, and I'll give it to you. I'll give you anything."

Fionn smiled. He traced Darius's cheekbone with a fingertip. "Anything?"

"Anything," Darius promised. He meant it. "I don't know how it is among your people. I don't know how you…"

"I'm not sure I believe your professions of ignorance in this case." Fionn stepped away, and Darius felt chilled, as if his touch had been a fire that had warmed him to the core. Darius followed him back to the river. Fionn stirred the ashes in their campfire, quickening the embers, then added more wood. It caught, and suddenly the small clearing was almost too hot.

Fionn set his boots down by the fire—he had walked barefoot back through the forest, unbothered by rocks and roots. His movements were slow but precise as he removed his tunic. The skin underneath was no paler than his face or hands, as if the sunlight didn't have any effect on him. Darius stood unmoving, staring at the smooth plains of his chest, the hollow between his collarbones.

Fionn gathered armfuls of leaves and moss and lay them against the base of a tree. After a moment, Darius realized what he was doing, and moved towards him. Fionn caught his hand and pulled him down onto the makeshift bed. It was surprisingly comfortable, and filled Darius's nose with the scent of the forest. Fionn smelled like that, but he also smelled like a young man. Fionn ran a finger along the hem of Darius's tunic, and he drew it off, responding to the wordless request.

"Why did you save my life?" Darius murmured into the quiet. They lay on their sides, facing each other.

Fionn traced the plane of Darius's chest, his eyes dark, a smile hovering on his lips. His hand came to rest against Darius's throat, fingers curving around the back, as if to feel the blood thrumming under the skin.

Darius covered Fionn's hand with his own. He trailed his fingers up his arm, marvelling at the fineness of the sparse blond hairs there. Fionn gave a shiver. Darius wrapped him in his arms, and drew him closer.

He knew what he wanted, but it wasn't possible. He didn't know if Fionn would understand—if he knew such a thing was done, or how it could feel. The closeness between them, in that moment, was everything, and Darius wouldn't risk frightening it away. He kissed Fionn gently. Even though he had kissed Fionn twice now, it felt far more transgressive to kiss him lying down. He remembered who he held in his arms—an enemy warrior, a member of a people whose ways and customs were so foreign that Fionn could be native to the moon. He felt a shiver of surprise and pleasure at the feeling of Fionn's tongue against his.

Their mouths fit together in a way that made Darius shake, and roused him to the point of pain. He felt lost in the sensation, almost afraid of the climax, sensing that something dark and unknowable awaited him on the other side. His restraint fell away, and he kissed Fionn fiercely, and felt his own desire matched at every instant—not only matched, for it was Fionn who had deepened the kiss, Fionn whose hand now reached down to open Darius's trousers and wrap around his cock.

Darius felt the shaking intensify. He was going to come from the sensation of Fionn's mouth on his, and the simplicity of his hand on his cock. He was not even moving his hand, but only squeezing slightly—perhaps he didn't know what to do, or how to give substance to his own desire. Darius wanted Fionn so fiercely that he began to think that even this innocent, unschooled touch could be enough to set him off, like a spark in a pile of dry kindling.

Fionn broke the kiss, and Darius felt the loss of his mouth as a physical pain. Fionn said something in his own language, the words short, slightly breathless. Then Darius realized, to his amazement, that his cock was wet—not only with his own desire, but with the oil Fionn had rubbed there, which he must have taken from the small jar that he had just tucked back into his pack—

Then Fionn was turning in his arms, drawing Darius, who responded half instinctively, behind him as he crouched, then pressing himself back against Darius's cock.

The silent command was unmistakeable. Darius pressed forward before he was even aware he was doing it, the tip of his oiled cock entering Fionn's body. Fionn let out a slight gasp, lowering himself onto his forearms. He pressed back against Darius in a way that was as sinuous as it was practiced.

Darius felt as if the world had reoriented itself.

He began to thrust, entering Fionn slowly, his astonishment subsumed by the aching pleasure that coursed through every vein in his body. He and Fionn moved together with a rhythm so natural and easy that it could have been their hundredth lovemaking. In every other sense, the experience was revolutionary, utterly different from anything Darius had ever felt. He felt as if he were understanding himself for the first time, as he lost himself in Fionn's body, in his attentiveness to every sound and movement he made.

Darius's hand went to Fionn's hip, the better to feel and anticipate his motions; his other wrapped around Fionn's cock. Fionn made another sound, almost a word, and then he breathed again, "Darius."

Darius was thrusting harder now. Fionn's gasps became cries. Darius's voice joined his, though he was not usually vocal during sex. He pressed forward, his chest against Fionn's back and his mouth at the space between neck and jaw, wanting to feel everything. He wanted to draw Fionn so close to him that their pleasure melted together, their hearts beat to the same time. He wanted to be inside him in spirit as well as body.

Fionn pressed against him, his cock hard and hot in Darius's hand. He moved with the same unselfconscious grace with which he did everything, whether loosing an arrow or lifting a cup, his body seeking pleasure without any hint of reticence or shyness. It was more intense than any other coupling Darius had experienced, but it was not just a question of skill—it was something that Darius could not articulate, in the throes of his passion. He pressed into Fionn so deeply that he lost all sense that there was anything else in the world.

Fionn's release, when it came, coursed through his body and into Darius. Darius followed in almost the same moment, coming apart inside Fionn in a rush of ecstasy that transformed him, and left him senseless as it receded.

They lay unmoving for several long moments. Darius could feel Fionn's heart thrumming through his back and into Darius's chest. He savoured every beat, as he did the sound of Fionn's ragged breathing, an echo of the pleasure they'd shared.

Finally, Fionn rose and pulled a blanket from his pack. Darius watched him, his eyes roaming over the lines of his body. He felt almost drunk with happiness. Fionn shook the blanket matter-of-factly and lay it over both of them. Then he drew Darius in for another kiss, twining one of his legs around Darius's and canting his hips slightly. Other lovers were blushingly awkward afterwards, or bashful, but it seemed these emotions were as foreign to Fionn as air to a fish.

Darius chuckled against his mouth. It felt impossible, what had happened between them. "Did I not satisfy you?"

"When I'm satisfied, you won't need to ask." Fionn rolled Darius onto his back and pressed their mouths together. The kiss was rough, an echo of the kiss Fionn had given Darius during that first transformation, before he had bitten him. Darius's blood heated, but after a moment, he broke the kiss, and took Fionn's face in his hand.

The other man gazed down at him, lips reddened and face flushed. His beautiful hair was woven with leaves that had the look of a savage form of crown. Darius brushed his lower lashes with his thumb—they were darker and fuller than those of any woman he had known. Darius scanned his face. Fionn wasn't easy to read, even in the afterglow of what they had shared, but Darius saw no regret in his eyes, nor even a hint of hesitation. There was lust, together with something that looked oddly like longing, but the sort of longing one felt for something lost and far away. Did Fionn regret that they would be parted tomorrow? Why? Darius felt no closer to understanding him than he had been before. If anything, learning of Fionn's desire for him had only added to the enigma.

The firelight touched Fionn's hair with gold and made his silver eyes glitter, and Darius smiled. He thought that if he spent a hundred years in Fionn's company, he would never tire of looking at him. He didn't think about the fact that they had only this night. He couldn't. Fionn returned his smile with an air of bemusement, as if Darius was as much an enigma to him.

Darius rolled Fionn onto his back and kissed him again, and again, and they swelled together like remembered song.

CHAPTER THIRTEEN

Darius woke the next morning to Fionn's mouth on his cock.

Pleasure was already rolling through him, and he instinctively cupped his hand around Fionn's head. Fionn's tongue circled the tip before pressing into it, deliciously teasing. Darius groaned. Fionn was far too skilful to be a novice. It wasn't the first time in recent hours he'd had that thought.

Fionn's mouth slid down his length, building a rhythm and then drawing back teasingly. Soon Darius was panting, his hand a fist in Fionn's hair. Finally, Fionn went down on him in earnest. Darius lifted his head, and the sight of Fionn crouched on all fours, giving him pleasure, was what sent him over the edge. He burst forth with a cry, and Fionn swallowed it all, drawing off slowly with a self-satisfied smile.

Fionn sprawled against Darius's chest, and Darius wrapped him in his arms, kissing the top of his beautiful head. He was trembling lightly, a bead of sweat running down his temple.

"I've grown unused to that sort of greeting," he said as he struggled to gain control of himself. The intensity of what he felt for Fionn was almost frightening. They had made love last night until the birds began to twitter in the trees, exhaustion finally causing them to collapse against each other, and yet Darius still wanted more.

"If that's true, you should be more discerning in choosing your lovers." Fionn allowed himself to be petted and kissed for a moment, then he rose and pressed his mouth to Darius's. His hands moved over Darius's body, teasing and stroking. Evidently, the previous night hadn't done much to dampen Fionn's enthusiasm either, or perhaps insatiability ran in his blood together with speed and grace. Eventually, his hands made their way down to Darius's cock, still soft from his earlier attentions. "What's this? Where's your Roman fortitude?"

Darius let out a sound that was half chuckle and half groan. "You haven't even given me a minute. Unlike you, I have no magical gifts."

"I want you." Fionn wrapped his leg around Darius's hip. And then, as if Darius might have missed his meaning, "I want you inside me."

"You should have thought of that before you opened your mouth." Darius murmured it in his ear. He felt delirious with pleasure. "Poor planning on your part."

"As you noted—" Fionn's lips moved to Darius's neck "—I lack the Roman gift for strategy."

Darius let out a breathy laugh. Somehow, though, he was growing hard again. He could have been sixteen, his body brimming with energy and desire. Except that he hadn't felt this way at sixteen, or any other time.

Afterwards, Darius wrapped an arm around Fionn, drawing him close so that his back rested against his chest.

The Celt made a soft sound of satisfaction. Darius pressed his face into his hair—it was like nuzzling warm cloud.

"I'm sorry," he murmured into Fionn's ear. "I didn't realize your people were so different from the other tribes. In Britannia, this sort of thing is outlawed. Worse than outlawed—I once saw a boy killed for it."

Fionn stiffened. But only for a moment. He leaned back against Darius, his fingers playing idly with the dark hair on his arm. "What makes you think it is any different here?"

Darius felt a chill. He drew back so that he was looking down into Fionn's silver eyes. "Then you—you're risking your safety by lying with me?"

"If any of my people knew of this, they would consider it a mercy to cut my heart from my chest. It's the fate that befalls anyone spirit-possessed, and driven to unnatural acts."

Darius recoiled, as much from Fionn's words as the calm manner in which they were delivered. "Spirit-possessed."

Fionn tilted his head. "Is my safety a concern of yours?"

"Yes."

Fionn smiled. The warmth in his eyes made Darius ache. "And only days ago, you tried to drown me in a river."

"I tried to throw you in a river. I'm not foolish enough to think I may have accomplished anything more." Darius brushed his fingers through Fionn's hair. "Come back to Sicily with me."

Fionn laughed. He kissed Darius affectionately. "Is that your home? Tell me about it."

Darius lay beside him. He told the silver-eyed creature in his arms about his beloved olive groves, how he had spent his childhood tending the land with his father. How it had been a lonely life, but not an unhappy one. How Fionn would enjoy wandering those groves, and the wilderness of scrub and pine beyond them, how the long, dry days of sunlight would warm him to his bones and couldn't fail to put colour in his cheeks.

Fionn listened with a slight smile on his face. "You love this Sicily."

Darius looked away, blinking. His eyes had grown unexpectedly moist. "Tell me about your home."

Fionn raised a brow. "I can, but I warn you, it is not so pleasant or idyllic as yours."

Darius waited. Fionn said, "My mother died when I was eight, my elder sister two years later. My father was devastated twice over. He is a great warrior, and she took after him. She would have made a much better heir than I."

"Your sister?" Darius said. "Then women can inherit among your people?"

"Yes. It is only the northern tribes who refuse to allow women to inherit property, though they still may inherit positions of leadership in certain circumstances. After my sister's death, my father took it upon himself to mould me into a fighter in his own image."

"He could scarcely have been disappointed in your abilities," Darius said.

"My father and I have never been friends," Fionn said. There was something in his voice that discouraged questions. "He and I are not alike, certainly not in the way he and my sister were. I suspect he would prefer to name my younger sister his heir, but I'm the eldest now, and the law is the law."

"You have one other sister?" Darius said. "Then she is the one who knows what you are?"

"As much as I," Fionn said. "Her name is Brigit. She is spoiled, cocky, and utterly bloodthirsty. Pray you never meet her."

There was an affectionate note in his voice. Darius smiled. "You are fortunate to have a sister. As a child, I often wished that my father would remarry and gift me with siblings."

"Why didn't he?"

"I believe the part of him that could love another died with my mother." He spoke plainly, voicing a truth he had scarcely allowed himself to think before now. "He had enough left in him to be a good father. And it was."

"It was what?"

"Enough." Darius thought of the sparse, quiet man who had raised him. A man who had always had an excuse to avoid company. Like Fionn, he had not been made in his father's image—far from it. And yet his relationship with his father had been filled with mutual respect, and a certain amount of curiosity. Darius realized that his father likely found Darius's love for company and yearning for adventure as much a mystery as Darius found his desire for eternal solitude.

"Tell me about your village," Darius said.

Fionn's silver gaze softened. He spoke of a lake framed by mountains, a raging river that tumbled and thrust its way to the vast western sea. Forests and fields through which he had gamboled as a child. Many of his reminiscences included Brigit, and Darius felt himself smiling as Fionn described a wild, golden-haired girl who sought to match Fionn in running and wrestling and every other physical pursuit, and when she couldn't match him, cheated her way to victory.

They made love again afterwards, and then they simply lay in each other's arms. The sun was rising above the trees—it was midday, Darius realized, his arms tightening around Fionn. He should rise. He should set out for Attervalis now to ensure he reached it before dark. And yet neither he nor Fionn spoke of it, as if by speaking the name of the fort they would hasten the moment when Darius would step through its mighty gates, and Fionn would melt back into the forest.

Darius didn't hear it at first. Fionn stiffened in his arms, and then he was sitting upright in a frozen posture, head cocked like a wary deer.

"Dress," he said shortly, springing to his feet.

Darius wasn't easily shaken from the embrace of pleasure and weariness, which dulled his soldier's instincts. "Fionn, what—"

Fionn had already pulled on his trousers. He tossed Darius his tunic. "They're coming."

Darius's other self, honed on battlefields and in midnight raids, slid back into place. He stood. "How many?"

"Four." Fionn was fully dressed now. He set to scattering the makeshift bed, tossing most of it into the river. "They saw the smoke."

Darius had lit the fire while Fionn drowsed that morning, just to get the feeling back in his toes. He wasn't a creature of the forest, unbothered by the cool damp, and it had seemed a harmless thing. Now he cursed his foolishness. At the same time, he became aware that four was not a force that should trouble Fionn, even if they were trained Robogdi assassins. The consternation on his face was because they weren't Robogdi, nor Roman.

It was because they weren't visitors he could fight—they were friends.

Darius swore again. If Fionn's people realized what they'd done...That was his first thought, before it struck him that he should also be worrying about his own safety. He cast about instinctively for his sword before remembering that he had lost it long ago.

Fionn seized him by the arm and pulled him, not gently, into the shadowy undergrowth. Darius dove into a bush, though it was one of the hostile thorny things that were forever catching at his clothing. There was no better symbol for Hibernia, he thought as he burrowed as deeply into the brambles as he could. The tribesmen should paint it on their shields.

Darius could now hear the approach of footsteps through the brush, the soft patter of voices. Fionn cast a last look about the campsite and then arranged himself on a rock with a bit of wood that he began carving. It was a settled, elegant pose that gave the impression of an hour's unbroken industry, and Darius was sure it would fool anyone who didn't look too closely—if they did, they would see the over-quick rise and fall of Fionn's chest, not to mention, Darius realize with a shiver of dread, the love mark his own lips had left on his neck.

They burst into the clearing a moment later—two large men and a reedy one of middle height, their hair varying lustres of gold. The reedy one was perhaps Fionn's age, or a little older, while the other two appeared to be in their thirties. From the rock, Fionn looked up and called out a calm greeting in his own language.

The men stopped. Fionn had seen them first, not surprisingly—he had an uncanny ability to blend into whatever wild backdrop he perched against. One of the men replied, surprise in his tone. The reedy boy smiled. Fionn rose, idly casting the stick aside and sliding the dagger into his belt. His posture was perfectly at ease.

The men came forward. One clasped his hand and then, curiously, kissed it, bowing his forehead over Fionn's long, graceful fingers. The other brawny one inclined his head and asked a question. Fionn responded dismissively, gesturing at the river. He gave the reedy young man a different greeting that had a note of warmth in it. The boy nodded, also inclining his head, though more shallowly than the others. His smile was amused, in contrast to the two older men, who both wore expressions closer to relief. Fionn spoke again.

Darius had no idea what excuse Fionn was giving the men for his absence from his tribal obligations—if Fionn had any obligations. Perhaps someone with his capabilities was given the freedom to do as he wished, and could simply flit through the woods as the fancy took him. But no—he had been among the Celts who had attacked Darius and his men on the riverbank after they fled Sylvanum. He had been part of the attack on the fort, though in precisely what capacity, it wasn't clear. Surely that meant he would have been missed during the past two days, not to mention all the time he had spent nursing Darius back to health.

Darius felt a familiar sense of frustration. Fionn knew Darius's full name, homeland, rank, and value to the Empire, not to mention his family's history, as short a story as that had been to tell. By comparison, Darius knew next to nothing about Fionn.

Another figure entered the clearing—Darius caught the flash of a golden head, paler than the men's. Whoever the forth visitor was, they seemed to be hiding behind the largest man, mischievously mocking their own smaller stature.

Fionn let out a pure peal of laughter that tugged at Darius's heart. Then he said in an exasperated voice, *"Brigit, meanne co conchora."*

At least, that was what it sounded like to Darius's unschooled ears. The figure—a teenage girl—leapt out from behind the man with a giggle. She was perhaps sixteen or seventeen, with a lean and willowy beauty. Darius would have known she was his sister even if Fionn hadn't spoken her name. Her colouring was darker, but her vividly blue eyes were the same shape as Fionn's, and her chin had the same stubborn sharpness. There was something of Fionn's grace in her build, though hers was more warm-blooded, having its origins in youth and the confidence of beauty rather than some fey mystery.

She leapt into Fionn's arms, wrapping him in a fierce hug. Then she paused and stepped back with a surprised, thoughtful look on her face. She looked Fionn up and down quickly, and then she glanced back at their partly dismantled camp.

Darius had to suppress a curse. There by the fire were two flat rocks bearing the remnants of the breakfast he had shared with Fionn. Brigit's eyes narrowed slightly. The mischief hadn't left her face, though now it was tempered by puzzlement. Her gaze lifted to scan the shadows.

Fionn murmured something to his sister with an edge in his voice, though he still wore a slight smile and stood relaxed among the others. To Darius, the mark on his neck was like a beacon, as was Fionn's rumpled clothing.

Darius forced himself to take a step back mentally, to examine Fionn with the eyes of an unknowing fellow tribesman who had happened upon him in the forest after he'd spent a night or two tracking Roman spies, or something equally explicable. The mark became a blemish, a bruise perhaps, and his rumpled clothing merely the result of a night spent sleeping on uneven ground. Darius felt certain from their easy chatter that these were conclusions the men drew.

Not Brigit, though. Her eyes roved over the place where Darius crouched, hidden by the darkness, and then returned to her brother.

Fionn took his sister's hand and led her from the clearing, and perhaps only Darius noticed the unnecessary firmness with which he gripped her, or the sharp look she gave him in reply.

He didn't glance back. A moment later, their voices faded into the rustle and song of the forest, and Darius was alone.

CHAPTER FOURTEEN

Darius remained in the bushes for another quarter hour. It was a strange feeling, crouched there with only the wind and the birds for company. Attervalis, he knew, was hours away—he was closer to his people than he had been in days, and yet he felt perfectly alone. It wasn't a comfortable feeling.

Finally, he left the underbrush and set off. The place where he and Fionn had lain was barely distinguishable—Fionn had effectively scattered the leaves and soft mosses. Abandoned in the early afternoon light, there was something gloomy and unwelcoming about the clearing now. Darius hurried along the riverbank as fast as he could given his limp.

The unwelcoming feeling only deepened the farther he walked. He felt as if the wall of green trees on either side of the river gazed down at him in disapproval, if not outright hostility. A bird darted across the water with a squawk, and Darius jumped. He moved quickly, for the river was broad and shallow here, offering flat banks scattered with stones to walk along, a much easier course than tramping through the forest.

Darius paused only once, to wash. As he rubbed the icy water of the river over his skin, he was met with evidence that the hours he'd shared with Fionn hadn't, in fact, been a dream. It wasn't that he wanted that. It was that it all seemed so unreal. He felt disoriented, as if Fionn's departure had broken some internal compass. A part of him wanted to turn and follow Fionn, if only to see him again, to prove to himself that he hadn't imagined his very existence.

Would he see him again?

Darius shoved those thoughts from his mind. What would his reception be at Attervalis? Rome had lost a fort under his command. It was a failure the like of which he'd never seen in his career, which with few exceptions had been one long string of successes—peace treaties negotiated; hostile foes set against each other, leaving Rome to pick up the pieces; chieftains charmed and placated until they came to understand the benefits of accepting the Empire's rule. Darius wasn't a general. He had little interest in battles, though he was competent enough at strategy. His skill was men—understanding the need that underlay the desires, and feeding that need. Darius didn't think that another man, in his shoes, could have prevented what had happened at Sylvanum, but that didn't lessen his guilt.

He became aware, suddenly, of the sound of voices up ahead. He had been walking for two or three hours—was he already nearing Attervalis? Darius slunk into the trees and crept towards the sound. His thoughts leapt immediately to Fionn and his companions—yet they had been heading in the other direction. And why would Fionn follow him? Angry at himself, Darius shoved the silver-eyed Celt from his mind.

As he neared the voices, he became aware also of a metallic rustling that he recognized immediately. He sheathed his sword and hurried on, no longer bothering to move quietly.

He came to a little hill. Below him was a clearing where a shallow stream broke off from the river, creating a broad, flat island devoid of trees. Upon this island was a cluster of Roman soldiers, their armour clanking softly as they moved. One man, whose bearing communicated command, stood a little apart from the main body, consulting with a man dressed in a scout's uniform. The others stood waiting, their faces wary and watchful. They hadn't yet noted Darius upon the hilltop—he stood in the shadows, his Celtic clothing blurred against the forest backdrop.

"Marcus," Darius called.

The name was half a question. Marcus standing there below him seemed nearly as improbable as his time with Fionn. Marcus turned away from the sentinel, his eyes squinting against the sun.

He gave a start, and his long face paled. "Darius!" he said. And then: "Gods!"

He surged forward, forgetting himself. He remembered before he reached Darius's side, and rather than embracing him, settled for a fervent clap on Darius's back. "Commander. By all the gods, where did you come from? Do you live?"

Darius managed a smile. Standing there with Marcus, gazing at his familiar, unshaven face topped with its uneven fringe of dark hair, stirred a curious mixture of emotions. On the one hand, he was relieved beyond words to see him; on the other, he had thought the man was dead. "As much as one can, in this unhealthy damp," he said. "I could ask the same of you, Captain."

"Commander, now." Marcus signalled to one of the other men. "Albinus is dead. I'm in charge of Attervalis. What's left of it."

Darius rocked back, and Marcus nodded at the look on Darius's face. "It's not a tale to hear standing up. Let's get back to the fort—I'll explain there." He signalled to his men. "We've lost them anyhow."

"Who?" Darius said.

Marcus shook his head, and let out a low laugh. "No you don't. You appear in our midst like something animated by Erictho, dressed up in barbarian robes—" He plucked at Darius's cloak—"and think you're owed answers first? I don't think so."

"I was injured," Darius said as they set off, the soldiers falling into formation behind them. Darius recognized none of their faces, and wondered again how many had survived from Sylvanum.

"Was the infection bad?" Marcus said, and Darius realized that Marcus, of course, with his keen eye for identifying an opponent's weaknesses, had already guessed the nature of Darius's injuries.

Darius hesitated. From Rome's perspective, there was no reason why he shouldn't tell Marcus about Fionn. And yet his instinct was to say nothing about him, to lead Marcus to believe that Darius had been healed of his injuries without assistance. But this was improbable, and Darius had no desire to have Marcus think him a liar.

So, Darius told Marcus most of what he had endured over the past days, though he said nothing about the supernatural elements, nor his last night with Fionn. He also didn't tell Marcus that Fionn was the frighteningly skilled warrior who had bested him on the riverbank; he implied that the Celt who had doctored him had been a stranger, his motives for helping Darius unclear. The last part was true enough, after all.

Marcus, to Darius's surprise, accepted his story without questions. "It's strange, of course," he said. "But who can understand the workings of an elf's mind? Naturally, some must be sympathetic to Rome's cause, and would prefer our rule to that of their savage kings."

Darius nodded, though he had grown less convinced of this in recent days. Marcus added, "Perhaps the man who helped you thought he could gain a bargaining chip for later use. I'm not sure it matters, though." His voice was heavy.

Darius looked him over. He might not be as adept as Marcus at measuring physical weaknesses, but he was a far better reader of human emotion. On Marcus's face, and even in his proud, graceful bearing, he saw not only fatigue but the ragged edges of a gathering despair. "How did you survive?"

"How?" Marcus raised his eyebrows. "I had nothing to do with it, I assure you. They didn't bother to kill me. After that grey-eyed demon knocked me over the head, I awoke on the beach, surrounded by corpses. I suppose the Robogdi assumed I was among them. Or perhaps the party that attacked us were Volundi—we've learned they have an alliance."

Darius said nothing. He couldn't tell Marcus that this wasn't news to him—even if he'd wanted to, there was no way to explain his ability to speak the language of a forest demon. Particularly to a man like Marcus, who was about as superstitious as a horse.

They reached Attervalis within an hour, moving swiftly through the diminishing forest. Attervalis perched on a rocky cliff overlooking the grey, unfriendly sea that stretched between Hibernia and Britannia. It was a mighty fortress, its high wall guarded by a sharp-tipped palisade. Darius had visited it once before, when he first arrived in Hibernia. It had been a comforting sight to approach by ship, punched into the green landscape like a fist, something sharp and practical and familiar driven into that alien place, dwarfing any fortress the Celts were capable of imagining.

"By the gods." Darius drew in a sharp breath.

Half of the southern wall had been obliterated. The sky was hazed with smoke—the line of brush near the fort was smouldering, as were several stands of trees that lay between it and the tree line.

Darius turned to his former captain and saw his own dismay reflected in his face, tempered by grim acceptance. "How were the tribes capable of this?" Darius said. "Not even the Turks ever managed to wreak this sort of havoc on our forts."

"The tribes weren't capable of it." Marcus's voice was even, his gaze distant. "But we were. Sylvanum was."

Darius let out a slow breath. "The onagers."

"The onagers, the missiles. They took it all. And put it to good use."

With difficulty, Darius clamped down on his horror, mindful of the soldiers watching. They had kept three onagers—high-powered catapults—at Sylvanum, along with an array of explosives and siege weaponry. It had been assumed they wouldn't need them, but Roman thoroughness forbade assumptions—the Empire knew next to nothing about Hibernia, after all, and it was possible that the natives were more advanced than their Britannian neighbours, perhaps even advanced enough to inhabit walled cities that would need to be broken. The notion that the Hibernians might capture a Roman fort and claim its store of weaponry for themselves had doubtless never entered the minds of the military strategists who had supplied the fleet.

The Celts weren't capable of matching Rome's firepower. So they had simply appropriated Rome's firepower. It was a strategy almost sinister in its simplicity.

"Do you think—" Darius stopped. "Do you think that was the plan all along? That the attack on Sylvanum was about more than destroying the fort itself? We don't store that sort of weaponry at Attervalis or Undanum."

"I don't see how they could have found out where we store our onagers," Marcus said. He let out a slow sigh. "Though I also didn't see how they could work out how to use them, and it seems they've managed that. You must teach me your gift of foresight, Commander. As you once reminded me, it was I who let the Trojan Horse into Sylvanum."

Marcus's voice was bitter. Darius saw the regret and self-recrimination in his face. He didn't try to argue against it, or insult Marcus's honour by claiming all the blame for himself. Marcus wasn't a child in need of coddling. Darius merely placed a hand on Marcus's shoulder, pulling him to a stop.

"Mistakes are part of the fabric of leadership," he said. "You'll make others, probably many, but you'll also have your successes. Your goal is to have the latter outweigh the former. No man has ever accomplished more."

Marcus gave a hollow laugh, but Darius could see that his words, as well as the warmth in them, had lightened the burden he carried. Marcus gave Darius a long look. "I am glad you aren't dead."

Darius laughed, though it sounded strange to his ears, tinged with exhaustion and something that he could only characterize as a *lostness*. "We've made progress, you and I."

"Yes, I'm sure it's quite the surprise to you that you've converted another man to your legion of admirers." Marcus's gaze held Darius's for a moment longer than necessary. "I have no doubt you'll acquire a few more, given that you can now add 'risen from the dead' to your reputation."

"Have I a reputation?" Darius said.

"Agricola talks of you often."

Darius smiled faintly at the mention of Agricola's name. He pictured the old man—though he was barely into his forties, Agricola seemed to have simply bypassed middle age—leaning over some map, grizzled brow lowered over those startlingly jewel-like eyes. When Darius had served in Britannia, he and the general would sometimes stay up late into the night, debating points of strategy. Agricola had insisted that Darius take the lead in any face-to-face negotiations with the Britannians. "We have an easy relationship. My father died several years ago, and I often saw him in Agricola, though they are nothing alike. I'm sure he speaks favourably of other men."

Marcus shook his head. "See, that's precisely what I mean. Do you know how many people see that dried-up bowl of pottage in a fatherly light? And no, he doesn't speak that way of other men. You seem to be the only one able to bring out that side of him."

Darius wondered what Agricola thought of what had happened at Sylvanum, and if he would still have the man's esteem. He followed Marcus into the fort.

Attervalis was laid out almost identically to Sylvanum, with its broad *via principalis* or central street, its forum and barracks and supply buildings. Darius felt like a ghost. The sense of lostness persisted—he wasn't sure if he felt lost himself, or if it was a feeling of lacking something vital. Every man he passed stared at the Roman in barbarian clothes, and some even did a double-take, no doubt assuming on the basis of his clothing and pale skin that he was a barbarian himself. Marcus paused to speak to two men in the principia, who he introduced to Darius as tribunes. Darius made the appropriate greetings and responded to the men's surprised welcome, though he barely heard his own words. Marcus led him then into the commander's house.

Darius almost wished he hadn't. Albinus's presence was everywhere—in the tidily arranged shelves; the rug of Venetian design; the small clay figurines on a table that had clearly been carved by a child's hand. He had only met the man a handful of times, but had respected his quiet competence. He knew Albinus's men had, too.

"He fell when the wall was breached?" Darius said.

Marcus shook his head. He poured Darius a glass of wine and handed it to him. "After. He led an attack on a Robogdi village, a place called Nestag, in retaliation for Sylvanum. We'd been reliably informed by one of our scouts that many of their warriors had gathered there after their attack on our fort."

Darius started. "Then the Robogdi bested you at their village?"

Marcus sipped his own wine. "No, of course not. It was a rout—they put up little resistance. Albinus took a knife wound to the stomach—not deep, but it became infected. He died within two nights." He paused. "Would you like to hear why we defeated the Robogdi so easily?"

"Isn't it obvious?"

"Oh, the elves have no discipline, no strategy—yes, that's true. But that night, there were no Robogdi warriors at Nestag. Not a one. Among the dead we found mostly women and teenagers, and a few old men. In the dark, our soldiers couldn't tell the difference."

Darius felt cold. "Then you destroyed a village full of women and children?"

"Yes." Marcus set his glass down on the table and strode to the window. "It was regrettable. The warriors must have caught wind of our approach, and abandoned Nestag, and their people, to their fate. A coward's choice, surely, but hardly surprising from men so wholly uncivilized."

"There are many words I'd use to describe the Hibernians," Darius said slowly. "Cowardly wouldn't be among them."

Marcus shrugged. He went on to detail Albinus's illness and the man's decision to place Attervalis in Marcus's hands, how he'd sent out scouting expeditions—including the one Darius had stumbled across—to try to track their enemies' movements. Darius was barely listening.

It didn't make sense. Darius didn't believe that Robogdi warriors would abandon their womenfolk to die in their place—not because he had any great respect for the Robogdi, but because it wasn't behaviour consistent with any race of men he had encountered, and Darius had encountered many. No. There was something else going on.

But what?

He thought back to the reports from before Sylvanum had been attacked, of how the Robogdi had gathered at Glyncalder, a settlement within marching distance of

Sylvanum, for their solstice celebration. He theorized now that this had been misinformation cleverly fed to their translator; the Robogdi had been gathering for an attack, using the solstice celebration as cover. He thought of the group of Celts captured so easily by Marcus. He thought too of the choice of weapon, nightfire, which not only robbed the Romans of their ability to fight, but their dignity. And how, as he now suspected, the Hibernians had somehow learned of Sylvanum's stock of weaponry, and had planned accordingly, attacking Sylvanum first and using their gains to cripple Attervalis.

There was a plot underway, Darius was certain of it. Somehow, he sensed the same devious mind at work. Darius wasn't the most skilful warrior, not did he excel at battle tactics, but he could read men. Agricola had valued him because of it. If all that Darius suspected was true, whoever was directing the allied Robogdi and Volundi forces was a dangerous man indeed. Darius had never known a barbarian mind capable of strategy, at least not to this degree.

What had Rome gotten itself into on this green isle?

And what was the strategy now? What possible motive could have led the Robogdi to abandon their women and children to slaughter? What did they gain from it?

Marcus seemed to have noted Darius's inattention. He motioned to the wine. "I'm not trying to seduce you. We have the food and drink checked daily."

Darius blinked, then gave a wan smile. He had forgotten he was holding a glass. "So. What is Rome's next move? Have you had word from Agricola?"

"We have, just this morning. Our orders are to strike the Robogdi and the Volundi hard. We have a supply ship on its way that will more than make up for the weaponry we lost at Sylvanum. Agricola is also in the process of reassigning one of the cohorts from Britannia to Hibernia. An additional five hundred men, together with the added firepower, will make for a suitable demonstration, Agricola thinks. Once we find out where their warriors are massing, we'll strike."

"A demonstration," Darius repeated uneasily. "Agricola wants to make an example of them."

"Naturally." Marcus eyed him. "You have concerns."

"A hard strike will close off any possibility for negotiation," Darius said.

"Negotiation? What is there to negotiate after the depravity of Sylvanum?" Marcus's tone was heated, but he checked himself. He regarded Darius with a wry smile. "But of course, you would still press for negotiation. But there does come a time, Commander, when talk is simply not an option. After Nestag, it is unlikely that the Robogdi will have a strong desire to negotiate with us."

"Then send messengers to the Volundi," Darius said. "Let us attempt to put a wedge in their alliance. Rome is not an unattractive suitor; there are many advantages we can offer. If nothing else, opening negotiations will buy us time to learn about these people. We know so little about the Hibernians, Marcus. I fear we are moving too quickly to deal with them—if we are underestimating their strategic capabilities, the results could be disastrous. We already have an example: Sylvanum."

Marcus sighed. He ran a hand through his hair, giving Darius a long look. "All right, all right. We can discuss strategy. But I will hear none of it until you've eaten."

He led Darius through the Commander's quarters to a spacious dining room simply but beautifully tiled with

Roman tesserae. A row of windows afforded a view of the sea, blue-grey beneath a cloudless sky and speckled with rocky islets. The shadows were deep; it was not long until evening. Marcus spoke to a servant, and soon baskets of the heavy bread gifted to them by the Darini were brought in, along with cheese, figs, walnuts, and roasted trout fresh-caught from a Hibernian stream. It was an odd repast, a mixture of Roman and Celt, but Darius had grown used to Celtic food in recent days, and welcomed both cuisines equally.

"I expected more survivors from Sylvanum," Darius said as they seated themselves. He tried not to allow the wrenching disappointment to seep into his voice. "Yet I've seen no familiar faces."

Marcus swallowed a mouthful of trout. "There are some. Close to one hundred. One of the surveillance parties I sent out today was mostly Sylvanum men—I've kept them together to avoid rejigging Attervalis's units."

"That's wise," Darius said.

"Among them is someone you may remember," Marcus said, a slight smile on his face. "I've already sent him a message about your return. He should be arriving shortly." Indeed, it was only moments before there was a knock at the door, and Scipio entered.

Darius's face broke into a smile. He embraced the other man without hesitation, then stepped back, uncertain if his gesture would be awkwardly received. But Scipio, fortunately, was smiling with the same easy cheer Darius remembered.

"Back from the dead, are you?" the older man said fondly but without overt surprise, and Darius thought back to the years they had spent together on campaigns in Gaul and Britannia. "This one's good at getting out of scrapes,"

Scipio added to Marcus. He pulled up a chair and helped himself to the food. "You should hear the story of his return to Isca Dumniorum after the natives held him hostage during trade negotiations. They ended up carrying him back to the fort in a litter after he used that honey tongue of his to convince them to accept less than they had been offered."

"You make me sound like a swindler," Darius said with a laugh. "As much as I was authorized to promise them, I promised. I simply presented it to them in a different light."

They fell into easy conversation, though Darius couldn't stop his gaze from drifting critically over Scipio. After all they'd been through together, he'd grown expert in reading the other man. He detected a heaviness in his posture that had not been there before, and wondered how much of it was due to Sylvanum.

"It wasn't the most noble of partings, was it?" Scipio said, in response to Darius's expression. "Never mind, man. It will make for a thoroughly tantalizing story one day, in some villa courtyard in the Albans..."

Darius surveyed him. "You are truly all right, my friend?"

Scipio gave a slight grimace, but the amusement didn't leave his eyes. "I hate to admit to it, but I have experienced greater embarrassment in my time, Commander. Wealth is not always a blessing in adolescence, admitting too many opportunities for debauchery...I only regret that I could not keep a sound enough mind to defend my colleagues, as you managed to do."

Darius looked away as the memories from that dark night surfaced. Scipio placed his hand on the younger man's shoulder, as Darius had done for Marcus. "Perhaps one day you or your cold-blooded captain can explain to me how one keeps one's head after swallowing a quantity of nightfire. Or do the brains of men like you share no blood at all with your nether regions?"

Darius smiled. "I wish I could claim such a thing. I was myself overcome by the drug, as you know."

"Yet you still managed to rescue what men you could. And one of those men—" He nodded at Marcus—"made it to Attervalis, and organized a search party that rounded up all the survivors it could, myself included. And there is also a story circulating of how you saved one of the men from being ravished, despite being under the influence of the drug yourself. You're not an unpopular figure among the soldiers."

Darius shook his head. "Any accolades they've chosen to bestow upon my memory are little deserved. I don't believe that resisting the urge to rape someone or being wounded by barbarians warrant acclamation."

"The men would rather follow you," Marcus said with his characteristic bluntness. "You're an experienced commander with a reputation established long before Sylvanum. They know you have Agricola's esteem. I'm green. The only reason I became commander of Attervalis is because the men above me were killed—or wounded, in the case of Albinus's captain, who's presently recovering from a nasty head injury in the infirmary."

"I hope you're not suggesting what I think you are." Darius raised his eyebrows. "Sylvanum's soldiers don't know me."

"They will soon enough. You've already won over every man you've spoken to."

Darius gave him a look. "I hope that our last...encounter hasn't coloured your opinion of me. I assure you, I'm not the Apollo you're implying. Please don't tell me your next words will be an ode to my eyes."

"Don't worry," Marcus said with a characteristic glower—and, Darius thought, a slight flush—"your modesty is safe from me. In any case, I'm not talking about your looks. It's the way you talk to people. You could win over the Emperor's wife and his lover both before dinner is served, and then have Augustus himself eating out of your hand before dessert."

Darius's thoughts turned, as they had with regularity since he'd left that shadowy grove, to Fionn, and the Celt's refusal to answer even the most basic questions. "My powers of persuasion are not universally effective, I assure you. And I have little appetite to take up a new command."

"Why not?" Marcus looked genuinely perplexed. "Surely your injuries are not so severe—"

"I'm well," Darius said. "It's—" He stopped. In truth, he didn't know what made him recoil from the idea of accepting another command. It wasn't because of Fionn. He certainly didn't relish the idea of hurting Fionn, and would make every effort to avoid it. He hadn't developed any warm feelings towards the rest of Fionn's race, though, and he knew his conscience would give him little resistance were he to meet any other Celt on the battlefield. Yet his experiences in the Hibernian wilderness had given him the sense that this was all wrong. Not just Agricola's orders, but Rome's very presence here.

Hibernia was not their world. It was a world of monsters and demons, and Darius couldn't begin to guess at the consequences they would face in trying to wrest from them this green island and place it into the Empire's cold, logical grasp.

Scipio was watching him. "The men don't blame you for Sylvanum, Commander."

"Is that it?" Marcus rounded on him. "And after that pretty speech you gave me about how I shouldn't blame myself for that mess?"

Darius rubbed his eyes. He swallowed his last bite of bread and rose. "Perhaps, gentlemen, we could discuss this further in the morning. It's been a long, strange day, on the heels of several long, strange ones. Surely you can bear the burden of command another night more, Marcus."

CHAPTER FIFTEEN

The next day, Darius managed to gracefully extricate himself from command—for the most part. Under the guise of safeguarding Marcus's dignity, he suggested that he share the position of captain with Scipio until they received further instruction from Agricola, which would likely come within a week or two.

Darius gave Marcus and Scipio an overview of his fears as far as the mysterious Celtic mastermind was concerned, though he managed to make only a dent in Marcus's skepticism.

"The nightfire was clever, no question," Marcus said. "But as to the rest, I remain unconvinced that the elves are mounting any sort of elaborate scheme against us."

"Even if they are," Scipio said, "what does it matter? Let them huddle in their trees and bogs and scheme. Once the supply ship reaches us, we will smash their schemes and their defenses for good."

Darius had no luck in convincing Marcus to send messengers to the Volundi. They could not have opened negotiations with the tribe without Agricola's approval, but they might have established unofficial communications with a tribe so mysterious that the Empire couldn't place even one of their villages on a map.

Five days passed at Attervalis in relative peace. Darius visited the fort's doctor, who pronounced himself astonished that Darius had healed himself of such a severe infection, the signs of which he could still see on Darius's body. Darius described the moss that Fionn had used on the wound, and the man grew even more astounded. He made Darius venture into the woods with him to identify the plant, whose miraculous properties he wished to study further.

Darius found himself surprised by how easily he slipped back into the routine of outpost life. The otherworldly days he had spent with Fionn, which amounted to about a fortnight, seemed little more than a dream. Yet the man himself never faded from memory. Unless Darius disciplined his thoughts, Fionn was forever interrupting them.

Even the smallest of things could bring him to mind. Darius would see his silver eyes in the glint of sunlight on the surface of the well; his ghostly hair in the churn of the sea as it struck the shore. At night, Darius's thoughts would turn to the feeling of Fionn's mouth against his, the pure grace of his body as it moved against Darius's, and he would pleasure himself in the darkness. This was new, and troubling—Darius rarely thought of anyone when he came at his own hand. Customarily, his desire summoned up some faceless, wide-hipped girl, or a leanly muscled torso. On occasion, he found himself resenting Fionn's intrusion into his life, which had opened up a part of himself that he hadn't known existed. A part, he thought, that wanted something more than this life of soldiering, and the sweet promise of his Sicilian groves. But what more there was, he didn't know.

Each time his thoughts drifted to Fionn, Darius would remind himself that the man was gone. They had parted, and would likely never reunite—the passion of their last night together amounted to an improbable dalliance, and a dangerous one at that. Fionn would slip from his mind, as he slipped into the forest depths.

And then, later, he would resurface.

It was because Fionn had left him with so many questions, Darius told himself. What was he? Why had he saved Darius's life? His inherent mystery made Darius doubt he would ever forget him, even if he did make it off this godsforsaken island. He would carry Fionn with him until the day he died.

He was only slightly surprised when, after a day spent around a table full of maps with Marcus, Scipio, and Attervalis's highest-ranking tribunes, Remus and Valens, Marcus knocked on his door.

Darius put his book aside and admitted the man to his room. It was a sparsely furnished space, and had formerly belonged to a tribune who had been reassigned to Undanum. It opened onto a little courtyard of unpaved greenery that had been left wild when the fort was built. The fresh breeze stirred Marcus's short hair, which was beginning to grow out, as he stood in awkward consternation at the threshold of the room.

Darius calmly seated himself on the narrow bed, leaving Marcus the chair. He didn't take it, but marched over to the courtyard door.

"The supply ship is nearing the coast," he said. "She should be in the harbour and ready for unloading in the morning."

"And our reinforcements?"

"The captain sent word that they will sail on a separate vessel in a few days."

Darius nodded. Despite sending out multiple search parties, they'd managed to find no trace of the men who had attacked Sylvanum or Attervalis. In fact, they'd found no trace of anyone. The two closest Robogdi villages stood empty—they'd even taken their animals. The Darini were no help—their feud with the Robogdi was longstanding, and they had little contact with the tribe, while the Volundi, with whom they had in the past formed a wary truce, had broken communication with them after they allied with Rome. The plan then was to burn the abandoned Robogdi villages to the ground and lay siege to Caervalle, a village nearly three days' march from Attervalis. After that, the Robogdi would be invited to treat with Rome. Refusal, or another attack on the Empire or her soldiers, would be met with further destruction.

They wouldn't refuse. No one ever did.

Darius waited until Marcus explained the real reason for his visit. Unfortunately, the man seemed eternally incapable of voicing his own feelings. "Our translator is to go aboard at first light and supervise the unloading."

Darius frowned. If Alaine, the mousey Britannian translator stationed at Attervalis, was being sent to the ship, it must mean it was manned by Britannian slaves—likely green ones, unused to Roman commands.

"I hear you requested a transfer," Marcus said. His back was still turned. "Scipio mentioned it accidentally—he seemed regretful afterwards, thinking you hadn't wanted the news out."

"It's all right." Darius had sent his request to Agricola on the same messenger ship that had departed Hibernia several days ago. "It wasn't a secret."

"Where will you go?"

Darius shrugged. "Wherever the Empire needs me."

"And then to your olive trees." Marcus's voice held amusement, but also something else. Darius had told him about Sicily, as he had told him other things during his time at Attervalis. They had spoken together far more freely, and comfortably, than they had at Sylvanum. "I have to admit, I've grown used to your presence at the briefing table."

"At your briefing table, you mean. You'll do just as well without me."

"Without your moralizing, perhaps," Marcus said. "Not without you." He examined Darius. "I've been meaning to ask about that. Did you come by that overbearing code of honour of yours after that experience in Gaul?"

Darius stiffened. "I'm sorry," Marcus said, grimacing at the look on his face. "Scipio said you didn't mind speaking of it—"

"It's all right." Darius gave him a wry smile. "Scipio is a dear friend, but not a particularly observant one. In truth, I don't know how to measure the effect my captivity in Gaul has had upon me, beyond the nightmares—which are far less frequent now." He considered the question, fighting back the clammy dread that arose whenever he allowed his mind to stray to that village square where he'd been held with his men. "Perhaps it made me more careful."

Marcus cocked his head. "About avoiding capture? I should think it would."

"No," Darius said thoughtfully. "About visiting similar brutality upon others as was visited upon me and my men."

"But you would never—"

"No," Darius agreed. "But there is, ultimately, only one way to kill a man, and unlimited ways to degrade his humanity. Duty may force me to the former, but nothing will compel me to the latter. For in doing so, I would degrade my own soul."

Marcus was gazing at Darius. When Darius met his eyes, he turned away, flushing, and went to stand by the open courtyard door as if to take the air. After a moment, Darius went to his side. He placed a gentle hand on Marcus's waist, an invitation for him to deny or accept, as he wished. After a long moment, the shorter man stepped back, leaning his weight against Darius's chest. Darius's arm circled his waist.

"I like your hair longer," he said. "It suits you."

"Don't." Marcus turned his head, meeting Darius's gaze steadily. "You've made your feelings perfectly clear. You care for me. You respect me. And that is where we begin and end. It's cruel to encourage me to hold out hope for more."

Darius let out a long breath. He didn't know what to say. He was used to this conversation, having had it a hundred times with a hundred partners, but not to the weariness that it caused him. Not weariness with Marcus, but with himself, with the trail of misery he always seemed to leave in his wake like refuse from a ship's hold.

Marcus seemed to read his thoughts. "How many lovers, I wonder, have watched that look of sadness pass over your face? How many despaired? Were any driven to acts of desperation?"

Darius winced at that last statement. Marcus was far too perceptive for his own good, or perhaps he had simply come to know Darius too well.

"Well, I won't be among them, as I think you know," Marcus said. "I can't imagine anything more tedious than pining, and you know I have a lavishly formed wife back home—as well as a talented lover—who will rally me back to myself if I do succumb. And yet you still won't fuck me." He scanned Darius's face. "There's someone else. Who?"

Darius didn't reply for a long moment. "There's no one else."

"Ah, but there is." The ghost of a smile crossed his face. "You ridiculously honourable fool. She's a fortunate lady. Or is it a lady? I find it difficult to guess your preferences."

"My only preference is to avoid hurting yet another man I've grown to respect."

"I give you leave to resume your former disrespect where I'm concerned, at least for tonight," Marcus said. Turning, he brought his mouth to Darius's.

Desire rose within Darius, warm and familiar. Yet with it came sadness, and a longing that couldn't be quenched by dark eyes and a sturdy, practical frame.

He pulled back to meet the question in Marcus's eyes. Smiling, Darius drew him back into the shadows and pushed him gently against the wall.

He sank to his knees, neatly drawing down Marcus's skirt as he did so. The other man's breath caught, but he recovered quickly from his surprise, and threaded a hand through Darius's hair. Darius used his hand first, teasing and stroking, and then wrapping the hand around Marcus's length. It was considerable, particularly given Marcus's smaller frame. Darius wetted the tip with his tongue, expertly teasing. His own cock began to swell, and he realized with a start that he was repeating the same pattern Fionn had followed that sweet morning in the grove. The longing struck him then like a thunderbolt, and left him empty and cold.

Fionn was gone. But before him was Marcus—Marcus, who had saved his life, who had become his trusted friend. Marcus, who deserved whatever Darius could offer him, as insignificant as it might be.

Marcus groaned. He cupped Darius's head, his eyes closing. Darius slid along his length, and it wasn't long before Marcus came in a rush, an involuntary cry slipping from his lips. Darius gently adjusted Marcus's skirt as he waited for the other man to recover.

"You've a rather chivalrous way of letting a man down," Marcus said once his breathing returned to normal. He caught Darius's hand as he sat upon the bed, drawing Darius with him. "Can I not do anything for you, Dari? Seems a mite unfair."

Darius smiled, kissed him. "You have, darling."

"You fear that it would mean too much to me," Marcus mused. "Isn't that it? I'm becoming adept at interpreting your code of honour. Well, I could send someone to you. Your lover, whoever they are, could hardly begrudge you taking your pleasure with a slave. That's perfectly harmless."

Darius stilled. "You have slaves here at Attervalis?"

"Yes—we house them out beyond the barracks. But I suppose Scipio and I have kept you to ourselves, haven't we? You haven't had much time to explore the fort." Marcus ran a hand through his hair. "They are mostly women. A few comely ones, though several of the men have grown rather fond of an odd little squinty thing who, I've heard, has some enthusiasm for their attentions. Not that I would know—as you've probably guessed, it's my view that women are for siring heirs on."

Marcus eyed him. "What is it?" Understanding dawned in his too-perceptive gaze. "Ah. You're a reformer, aren't you? You would be. Well, you can rest assured that the slaves we've taken have been well-treated. The men may only take their pleasure on the ones who are willing. A number of them are, as the men gift them with food and trinkets in return for their affections. Their families were fairly compensated. Albinus was scrupulous in this area— but then, he was a Stoic. We've had a steady trickle of Darini seeking to auction off superfluous daughters."

Darius didn't reply. He supposed he was a reformer. He disliked slavery, certainly, and his father had been a reformer, or so Darius had always assumed, for he'd only used hired freedmen to work his groves. In truth, though, Darius had never given the matter much thought—slavery was part of the foundation of the Empire, and simply one of the many unpleasant realities of life.

He thought of a roomful of blonde Celts, chained and bound. He thought of Fionn among them, all that proud courage and malevolence and tenderness forced to bow to a master's will. The image left him unsteady, it was so wrong.

"They treat their slaves far worse than Rome, you know," Marcus said. "The Robogdi cut off their hands if they try to escape, while the Darini chieftain regularly sires bastards on his and then has them executed when they lose their figures. They have no laws in this area; they follow their own brute natures."

Darius was barely listening. His fears were irrational—Fionn would never allow himself to be captured, and it wasn't as if his people would sell such a valuable asset. Yet he couldn't push them away. He vowed to visit the slaves and examine them regularly to ensure that Fionn wasn't among them.

At the edge of Darius's mind was the awareness that his fear wasn't only irrational but tinged with the faintest of hope. But he pushed those thoughts away. Fionn was gone.

Marcus was watching him with a frown. "Shall I send you someone? By the gods, Dari, you look like you could use it."

Darius forced a smile. "No thank you, Marcus." He ran a hand though his hair and let out a humourless breath of laughter. "You were right. There is someone else, in a way. I find that I—I can't stop thinking about him."

"What, don't tell me he turned you down." Marcus let out a sharp laugh, and then he fell silent, wincing. "Sorry, Dari. That was unkind. It's just difficult for me to comprehend anyone rejecting your affections."

"One day, darling, I am going to fall off that pedestal you have me on, and then you will have to find someone else to worship."

Marcus shook his head wryly. He kissed Darius on the cheek. "Very well. I'll leave you to your moping. Only don't drive yourself to any acts of desperation, please. Remember what I tell myself."

"What's that?"

"Every life has its share of miseries," he said. "If not heartbreak, they would come at you in some other form."

"Thank you. That will certainly help me fall asleep tonight."

Marcus laughed, and then, after kissing Darius again, he left.

Darius sat there, gazing out at the green boughs that waved in the breeze. Then he stood and went out.

The soldiers he passed bowed their heads, many with smiles or a joking comment. Darius had made it known, as he did in every company he led, that he had no use for unnecessary stiffness. A commander should be respected by his men, it was true, but that respect shouldn't get in the way of camaraderie. Darius, despite his distraction, met every smile and comment, clapping those he had worked with on the shoulder. He stopped to speak quietly to a man whose lover had been stationed at Sylvanum and had not been among the survivors.

When he finally reached the outbuilding Marcus had described, he found it guarded by two men playing at cards. They jumped to their feet as Darius approached. He raised an eyebrow at the cards to make his disapproval clear, but chose not to deepen their embarrassment by commenting. "Gentlemen. I've come to inspect the slaves' condition."

The men, still flushing slightly, exchanged a knowing look. "Of course, Comman—ah, Captain." One of the men held the door open, and Darius stepped through.

He found a roomful of women staring back at him. None seemed to be beyond their thirties, though there were few who looked especially maidenly—the youngest, a pale redhead with startling black eyes, was perhaps twenty-five. All ripe, all beautiful in that watercolour Celtic way. But not a child among them.

In Darius's experience, barbarian families usually sold children, having too many. Sometimes you came across a man seeking to sell off his barren or frigid wife, but surely that couldn't be the case with all of them?

The redhead rose, her lips slightly parted. The women weren't bound in any way, but lounged freely upon cushions and crates strewn across a floor of rushes. The windows were open; there was a table with several jugs of water and a picked-over plate of bread, berries, and hard Celtic cheese. None of the slaves bore any evidence of rough handling. All in all, it looked like a comfortable situation, as Marcus had assured him.

The redhead, though pretty enough, had a squint, and Darius guessed she was the one Marcus had alluded to. The one who not only bore the men's attentions, but enjoyed them. She was a little skinny for Darius's tastes, though he couldn't deny that her features were pleasing, as was the flirtatious slant of her mouth.

She touched his hand gently and lowered her lashes, scanning him from head to toe and pausing noticeably on a certain area.

"Sir," she said, the Latin word lisping through her thick accent. With her free hand, she mimed something quick but perfectly unambiguous. "Please?"

Darius drew his hand back. He forced a smile. "No thank you. I merely came to check on your condition."

The woman kept smiling. She hadn't understood a word, of course. But there was something in her smile that made the hair rise on Darius's neck. It wasn't mockery, nor amusement at his seeming shyness.

It was pity.

Darius's gaze drifted over the women. Many of them were blonde, and one was almost as pale as Fionn. She met his gaze with eyes that were blue, not silver, and tilted her head in curiosity. Her pale waves stirred at the gesture, and Darius remembered the softness of Fionn's own hair, the way it slid through his fingers like rushing water. He saw the pale, winged creature he had become, watching his with unknowable eyes.

He inclined his head at them, keeping his expression composed. Then he slipped out.

*

Darius spent several minutes questioning the soldiers, now shame-faced and alert. When had the women come to the fort? Had they been all brought by their families? What were the reasons given for selling them to Rome?

He was unsurprised when the soldiers claimed that no one had questioned the women's families—they wanted gold, one of the men said with a shrug. They always wanted gold—what was mysterious about that?

Darius paced back to his room, unsatisfied. He had half a mind to summon Marcus to him again, but he didn't know what he would say. He had felt this unease before at the presence of a group of Celts in his fort.

Yet these were not warriors taken prisoner under mysterious circumstances, but women fairly bought and paid for. Darius wondered if his failure at Sylvanum was casting a shadow on Attervalis, and he felt a chill at the idea that he might not be able to trust his instincts anymore.

But perhaps it was true. He had been through so much. Perhaps it had taken a toll. It did seem ridiculous, in the warm lamplight of his room, that he should be suspicious of a roomful of women.

Darius settled for doubling the guard on the women, and ordering them to be searched daily from head to toe. Then he stripped and threw himself on his bed, hoping for sleep to take him soon, and also that the days between now and his removal from Hibernia would pass swiftly.

CHAPTER SIXTEEN

Darius was awoken an hour before dawn by pounding on his door.

He rose and spoke briefly with the soldier outside. Smoke had been spied offshore, but in the darkness, the source couldn't be identified. Marcus had ordered all senior officers to the briefing room.

Darius splashed himself with water from the basin and threw on his clothes. He felt a building sense of grim inevitability. The shadows beyond his door seemed darker, somehow, as if they had been joined by shadows from the deep woods the Empire had hacked away to build her forts.

"Report," Darius said unthinkingly as he entered the briefing room.

Marcus looked up. "We think it's the supply ship."

Darius felt the foreboding grow, morphing into a presence that took up space in the room.

Scipio raised an eyebrow. "You don't look surprised."

Darius rubbed his face. "Have we had word from the ship since last night?"

"No," said Remus, one of the centurions. His hawkish gaze was preoccupied with the sailing charts upon the table. "Given that the tide has turned, they should have put into harbour several hours ago. Something's wrong."

"Where is the translator?" Darius said.

"Alaine? He set sail last night, as soon as the ship was sighted on the horizon," Marcus said. "They were waiting offshore until the tide was favourable. He felt it would be easiest for all involved if he went aboard and prepared the men for unloading."

Darius frowned. "Was that necessary?"

"It was his idea. He's a man who knows his business."

"Is he?" Darius had spoken to Alaine only twice since arriving at Attervalis. He couldn't say he'd gotten a handle on the man at all. He was small and dark-eyed, typically Celtic, and though his Latin was understandable enough, he always gave Darius the impression that he had little desire to make friends, and disliked being pressed into conversation. Darius had encountered enough men of that temperament to know that if you could get them talking about their own interests, you could often form a bond with them despite themselves. But he'd had no luck with the reedy Britannian. That the man had sailed out to meet the supply ship shortly before it caught fire struck Darius as an unpleasant coincidence.

"We should send out a rescue vessel, Commander," Scipio said. "If they're unable to get the fire under control, they'll be swimming to Attervalis."

"What rescue vessel?" Marcus said. "All we have is the *Daedalus*, and that old trireme doesn't even have hoists — we'll be fishing men out of the water with nets."

"Gentlemen, I know the situation is urgent, but can we back up a step?" Darius said. "Marcus, how well do you know Alaine?"

Marcus gave him a sharp look. "I know that as long as he's paid promptly and out of all proportion to his worth as an uneducated barbarian, he's tractable and quick to take direction. Why?"

Darius drew a breath. "I believe we have to entertain the notion of foul play."

Remus let out a breath of laughter. Marcus said nothing, merely watched Darius with a furrowed brow.

"Foul play?" repeated another centurion, a bulky man named Aeneas. "We aren't even certain if there's a fire on that ship, or if some onshore smoke has drifted out to sea."

"If it's the *Minerva*, it probably started in her kitchen," Remus said dismissively. "I've seen enough of that in my time. Those old galleys are infamous for fires—the *Minerva's* had two in her day. They smoke like hell, but they're easy to contain. There's no reason to think she's in danger of foundering."

Darius took a slow breath to control his temper. "Perhaps it is a kitchen fire. Perhaps the ship's cook set the porridge alight. If so, no further thought is necessary beyond rescuing the men. If, on the other hand, this was an act of sabotage, then we have a serious situation on our hands."

"Alaine dislikes the Hibernians," Marcus said. "Most Britannians do. He views them as primitive backwater-dwellers, unlike our cosmopolitan barbarians on the larger isle, who have long traded with the continent and know something of the wider world. Even among barbarians, there are hierarchies. I can't imagine him helping them."

Darius was momentarily stymied. Part of him was astonished at how dismissive these men were towards any suggestion of Celtic strategy after Sylvanum — not to mention the destruction they'd wrought on Attervalis. And yet hadn't he once been of the same mind? For most soldiers of the Empire, the sub-human intellect of the barbarian tribes compared to Roman ingenuity was as self-evident as the wetness of water. It wasn't easy to divest oneself of such deeply-held truths. Even Darius found himself recoiling from his own theories, and he knew for a fact that intelligent Celts existed — he'd spent hours conversing with one. Fionn might lack any knowledge of philosophy — nor to mention ethics — but he had a mind as quick as his sword arm.

He knew he had to keep trying to convince these men. "Nonetheless," he said. "We can't overlook what happened at Sylvanum. There was planning there, Marcus, and there may be planning here. We can't look upon these people as simple-minded. We must take them seriously if we want to avoid another disaster." He could hear his voice growing heated, which was most unlike him.

Marcus said nothing for a long moment, his eyes on Darius. He finally sighed. "What would you have us do, Captain?"

"Send patrols into the forest," Darius said. "A show of force. Whatever the Celts are planning, make it clear that they won't be able to carry it out easily. Double the sentries along the wall. And send men — in rowboats, if need be — out to that ship so we can work out what the hell is going on."

Marcus nodded. "Scipio, draw up the new duty roster. This will mean long hours, and the men won't be happy about it. Tell them that Agricola in his wisdom has seen fit to bump up their pay — that should keep them quiet enough."

"Has he?" Remus said.

189

"No, but I believe he'll be amenable. After all, Rome has been saving on salaries considerably since Sylvanum was wiped out." Marcus said it in a flat voice. "Remus, you take a party down to the harbour. Send out as many boats as you can. Have blankets ready, in case there *are* men overboard—those waters are cold, even at this time of year."

The men filed out, and Darius was left alone with Marcus.

"Thank you," he said. "I know you're not convinced about this."

Marcus shrugged. "I trust your instincts, Dari. It's really as simple as that." He smiled slightly. "You didn't tell me to station additional guards around the well."

Darius gave him a long look. "Because I know you already have."

Marcus made a sound that wasn't quite a laugh. "True. But these theories of yours have me wondering if perhaps I should double them."

*

Morning ushered in another warm, cloudless day, as well as the news that the *Minerva* had foundered. Remus managed to rescue thirty-two men—all Roman, as the Celtic slaves had been kept in chains below decks and were presumed dead. In total, nearly eighty souls had been lost.

One of the cooks was among the rescued, and protested until his voice grew hoarse that the fire had begun in the cargo hold, not the kitchen, though he had no idea what had sparked it. The *Minerva* had been carrying a large quantity of explosives, and it was possible that improper storage had been at the root of the ship's destruction.

"What do you think?" Scipio said. He, Darius, Marcus, and Remus stood on the practice grounds, which had been cleared of vegetation and hard-packed but somehow still managed to accumulate a smattering of weed and shrubs. "Do we send to Agricola for more supplies? There was a considerable array of weaponry aboard that ship. The general may not be able to spare more at present."

"We have to send him news of the ship's fate regardless," Marcus said. He ran a hand through his hair. "I don't know if I can venture to provide advice on how to proceed. Perhaps we may leave it up to the great man to make that determination himself."

"So much for our hard strike against the Robogdi," Remus said heavily. His short hair was disordered from much wind and salt water, and his arms were bandaged from where he had cut himself sifting among the wreckage of the *Minerva* for survivors. "Will Agricola bother sending the promised five hundred soldiers if we lack the weaponry to carry out our plan?"

Marcus rubbed his face. "The general was already reluctant to reassign those men. He worried it could leave him shorthanded. The Britannian natives are not all peaceable—those in the west have been restive lately."

"The west," Darius murmured. "Isn't that where Alaine was from?"

"Do you still suspect him of sabotage?" Remus said. "The man is dead, Commander—I mean, Captain. It's likely he was down in the slave hold with his countrymen when the ship foundered."

"And now we lack a translator," Scipio said.

"That is the least of our worries, unfortunately," Marcus said. "I suppose I should begin composing my report to Agricola. Darius, if you could assist me? I suspect the old man will react more proportionately to this news if he hears it written in your voice."

Darius moved to follow Marcus to the Commander's quarters, but before they had travelled a dozen steps, a tremendous *boom* nearly threw Darius off his feet.

"What was that?" Darius shouted up at the wall. The nearest sentry turned and shouted something down at them that was lost in another ear-splitting *boom*.

"It's the onagers again," Marcus said, then let out a string of curses. "I thought we killed enough of those bastards last time that they wouldn't try another attack. Perhaps you were right about the *Minerva*, Commander. Their timing is uncanny—as if they knew we'd right now be reeling from the loss of the ship."

Another *boom*. "That's the north wall," Darius said. He and Marcus set off at a gallop.

It was as Darius feared. One of the parapets had been smashed, and though Darius saw no bodies, he heard shouts and screams from the other side of the wall. The soldiers manning the parapet had fallen, but at least some were still alive. Darius didn't think. He shouted for the closest soldiers to accompany him, then led them through the north gate to the rubble. They fished out the wounded men (one was dead, the other three badly wounded), and dragged them back into the fort before the next missile struck.

Darius risked a glance over his shoulder before the gate closed behind him. The forest was a number of yards away across a field of green. He could just make out the figures of men darting among the shadows—more men than he would have expected—and a hulking shape that he guessed was the onager.

"Marcus!" he shouted, once he'd handed off the wounded man he was supporting to another soldier. "The onager is just past the tree line. If we can send a party to surround them from behind—"

"It won't work," Marcus said, turning from the soldier he'd been giving orders to. "The terrain drops off steeply in that direction—we'd be fighting uphill."

Darius thought that over. "Then we attack them head-on. They can't have more than a few dozen men, surely."

"Try a few hundred," Marcus said grimly. He motioned to the western parapet. "That's Terius's estimate, and I believe him. The man has the eyes of an eagle."

Darius closed his eyes briefly. He knew what this meant. "Nevertheless, we must meet them. We can't allow them to continue pounding away at our walls."

"I beg to differ, Captain," Marcus said. His face was pale, but his voice was determined. "Walls can be rebuilt. Men cannot. If we join them in battle in that forest, with the numbers they have, we will likely win—but the cost will be steep. We lost too many men today. I won't allow this bloody tide to continue. That's why I'm going to send word to Undanum."

"Reinforcements?" Darius said. "But that will leave Undanum undermanned."

"It's of little matter. Undanum has a strategic advantage, having been built upon open ground. The Celts haven't targeted them, nor are they likely to. Once those men arrive, we'll set fire to that forest and wait for the rats to scurry into our grasp." Marcus's hand was clenched on his sword, and with a seeming effort, he loosened it. "Our rider will reach Undanum within two hours. The men will be here by evening. Our walls can hold until then, Dari."

Darius didn't argue. The truth was that he was as eager as Marcus to spare Roman lives. It made sense from a strategic perspective as well—men were a resource as much

as weapons were, and after the twin disasters of Sylvanum
and the *Minerva*, it was a resource in short supply.

Darius spent the rest of the day overseeing the
archers. He was no better at shooting than he was at
swordplay, but he knew how to manage men, especially
men jittery from recent setbacks and discontented with their
commander's decision not to fight the enemy. He identified
the malcontents and kept them apart from the other men,
speaking to each separately so as to allow them to voice their
concerns. He gave the same leeway to the less excitable
soldiers, though he put a stop to any discussions critical of
Marcus. Happily, the archers had some successes; over the
course of the day, they picked off over fifty Celts, despite the
difficulty presented by the distance and the tree cover.
Darius encouraged them to make a competition of it, and as
darkness fell, some of the men were joking with each other.
The onager had ceased firing—the missile strikes had
lessened considerably over the afternoon, so much so that
Marcus believed the Celts were running out of ammunition.
Darius wasn't so sure. He knew what Sylvanum's stores had
held, and unless a substantial amount had burned with the
fort—possible, he supposed—there was no tactical reason
why their fire should have lessened. Surely the Celts would
have no qualms about wreaking maximum damage upon
Attervalis.

It was as he was heading down to join Marcus and
the other senior officers for a hasty supper that he
remembered the women. He doubted that, given the gravity
of the situation, anyone would have bothered keeping up
the guard. Sure enough, he found the outbuilding
abandoned.

Darius muttered a curse. He wondered how he was
going to convince Marcus to maintain a guard on a roomful

of whores during a siege. He pulled the door open, expecting to be confronted with a sea of confused and alarmed faces, as prettily painted as they had been before.

The room was empty.

Darius's heart hammered. Had the women been moved? If so, why? The outbuilding was well outside the range of the onager. He stood there for a few seconds, staring, as if he expected the women to materialize before him. Then he went out.

"Soldier," he called to the first man he saw. He was leaning against one of the storehouses in an odd way that made Darius wonder if he'd been injured. "Where are the slaves? Why was I not informed that they had been moved?"

The man turned, and Darius froze. Staring out at him from beneath an ill-fitting helmet was the red-haired wench who had propositioned him. Her luxurious locks were stuffed into the helmet and her figure was concealed by a soldier's cloak. She looked startled, and then her gaze flicked past him, and she smiled. She puckered her lips in a lascivious kiss.

"What are you—" Darius began.

"Sir, look out!" a voice cried.

Darius ducked instinctively. A sword sliced through the air above him. He rolled in anticipation of another blow, colliding with the red-haired woman, who fell on top of him. He moved to shove her off, but she was on him like a wildcat, rolling him onto his back before he could recover his bearings and drawing a dagger from some hidden place in her stolen uniform. She brought her face close to his and hissed something, her gaze full of triumphant fury.

Darius knew he had to strike her, but his entire being recoiled at the prospect of doing so. Instead he knocked her arm aside, hooked his leg around her, and forced her onto her back. She was strong, and managed to jab his shoulder with the tip of her blade. He let out a hiss of pain, and they wrestled for a moment, before she gave a cry of pain and went still.

Darius's grip loosened and he gazed down at her, worried he had hurt her. In that same moment, she gave him a feral grin and shoved him off her. Then she was on him again, dagger raised for a killing blow.

It never came. Someone wrenched the woman off him, then threw her hard against the wall. Her head, having lost its helmet during the scuffle, struck the stone. She went down and did not move again.

Marcus loomed above him. "By the gods, that was pathetic."

"I didn't—" Darius was out of breath. "I didn't want to hurt her."

"That was what I meant." Marcus helped him to his feet. "You're going to have to abandon your squeamishness on that front, and fast. Look."

Darius followed his gaze. There against the open door of the building that had held the women lay the motionless form of a Roman soldier. Blood pooled beneath him, and his sightless eyes were wide. Against the building lay another unmoving body—a woman. She too was dressed in soldiers' garb. A sword lay beside her, and another was impaled in her chest.

"That was the one who attacked you first," Marcus said. "The soldier stopped her before she could try again. He cut her down, yet even in her dying throes she still managed to deal him a death-blow. Do you still feel chivalrous?"

Darius recoiled. And yet he knew some of the Hibernian tribes trained their women for war, and allowed them to fight alongside the men. He had seen it, after all, yet still it shocked him.

"You were right, it seems," Marcus said. He began to run, hauling Darius behind him. "Damn you, but you were right. They opened the gate. We managed to get it shut again, but not before they let in two dozen warriors."

"Have they been dealt with?" Darius demanded. Marcus only fixed him with a grim look. Darius soon saw the reason for it. As they crossed the *principia*, Darius heard the sound of fighting.

Behind the officers' quarters, their backs to the northern gate, ten Celtic men fought like madmen, their golden hair gleaming, their daggers slashing. Darius drew in his breath.

Robogdi assassins.

Bodies lay scattered across the ground, most of them Roman soldiers. The Robogdi were making a fearsome racket, their characteristic ululating battle cry echoing off the walls of the fort. The Roman response was disorganized — the Celts had clearly taken them by surprise — but it was nevertheless obvious that the Robogdi were losing. As Darius watched, archers came racing along the wall and opened fire, downing two Celts.

Marcus moved to join the attack, but Darius gripped his arm.

"What?" Marcus demanded. There was a wild look in his eyes. The slaves' treachery had rattled him, and Darius knew he wasn't thinking clearly. If he had been, he would surely have seen what Darius could.

"Listen to them," Darius said. "This is a distraction. But what are they distracting us from?"

Marcus stared at him stupidly for a moment, then his expression cleared, and Darius could see him begin to think.

"I don't know if we killed all the women," he said. "I didn't have time to count."

Darius's hand tightened on his arm as he became aware of something else. "Do you smell smoke?"

Marcus whirled and shouted for two of the soldiers standing at the edge of the fray to follow. They raced to the eastern gate—the gate that was only used to allow the sentries to pass in and out during their surveys of the rugged coastline below. The gate that would only be threatened if the Celts managed to climb up the partly sheer cliff face...

One of the storehouses was on fire. Darius paused to give orders to the soldiers who had leapt into disarrayed action to save it, emptying buckets of water against the building that did little to quench the inferno. Darius got them focused instead on creating a firebreak between the storehouse and the neighbouring buildings—the storehouse was already lost. Marcus watched him doing it—there was a glazed look on his sunburnt face, and Darius could see he was giving in to shock. Darius didn't blame him. That the Hibernians would plan out an attack this sophisticated—placing their women warriors in Roman custody slowly and benignly enough not to draw suspicion...The Darius who had sailed into that Hibernian harbour all those months ago would not have believed it possible.

And yet it had all happened before—at Sylvanum. Another group of Celtic prisoners, another Trojan Horse. Darius sensed the same hand guiding this attack, the same savage intellect.

If he ever met the man responsible, Darius would kill him on sight.

Darius grabbed hold of one of the tribunes as he raced by, failing to recognize Marcus and Darius in the chaos.

"Find the women," Darius ordered. "Comb the entire fort until every one is accounted for, and put to death."

"But sir, the fire—"

"Will be the first of many if we don't put those women down," Darius said gravely. "Gods know what other mischief they will get up to. You have my permission to assign as many men to the task as need be. Do it quickly, soldier."

"Sir." The man saluted him, and raced off.

Marcus and Darius ran to the eastern gate. But as they neared it, a red-haired Celt charged them, screaming.

Darius barely had time to put his sword up. Fortunately, Marcus knocked him out of the way and took the brunt of the Celt's attack, dispatching of him with neat brutality.

"By the gods," Darius said as Marcus helped him to his feet. The gate had somehow been shattered, and through it poured wave after wave of Celts. Most of the Roman guards lay dead, their bodies scattered over the threshold, though several archers still fired valiantly from the walls.

Darius seized the arm of a Roman soldier in retreat, his face glazed with panic. He looked barely twenty. "How did this happen?" he demanded.

The man stared at him unblinkingly, as if he'd forgotten who Darius was. Then he seemed to start back to himself. "Sir—when we heard the Robogdi break through the other gate, and the fire, half the guards went to provide assistance. That was when they fired the explosives—"

"Explosives?" Darius repeated. "Another onager, you mean?"

The man shook his head. The tide of Celts had been temporarily stemmed by a half-dozen soldiers, but Darius could see they couldn't hold it long. "They had something else. I don't know what, but it went off like blaststone against the gate."

"Blaststone," Darius said. "But that's impossible. How could they get their hands on—" He stopped, a sick feeling rising in his stomach.

"The *Minerva*," Marcus said grimly. "She carried a quantity of blaststone in her hold."

Darius swayed. The Robogdi or Volundi—he supposed it made little difference which—had managed to board the *Minerva* and offload at least some of its weaponry before it sank.

Or, rather, before they sunk it. There could be no other explanation.

"Will our reinforcements arrive soon, Commander?" the man said, unthinkingly directing his question at Darius.

Darius looked at Marcus. He saw the same thought reflected in the other man's eyes. The reinforcements from Undanum were not unduly late, but it was ominous that they were late at all. Had they too fallen victim to the Celtic mastermind's preternatural ingenuity?

Darius had no more time to ponder it. The Celtic warriors broke through the line of Roman guards, slicing them open in a spray of red. More soldiers ran forward, joining the fray, but it made little difference. Dozens of warriors poured through, and Darius could see no prospect of stopping them. Their yellow hair was like a river of gold, their daggers flashing like moonlight on waves.

It made no sense, in that moment, for Darius to think of Fionn. His eyes had been like the flash of those daggers, gleaming at Darius out of the night. These warriors were his race, his allies, and they were here to destroy Attervalis. Somehow, Darius's memories of Fionn, his hair and laugh and alien eyes, melted together with the river of invaders, a grand kaleidoscope that resolved into one hard reality: it could all end here, tonight.

Darius met Marcus's gaze. Then, together, they drew their swords and stepped forward to greet the conquerors of Attervalis.

Thanks for reading!

Darius and Fionn's story continues in:

The Forest King (Green Labyrinth, Book Two) — Available now!

The Soldier Mage (Green Labyrinth, Book Three) — Coming Spring 2020

Made in the USA
Monee, IL
20 December 2021

86538982R00121